W9-CLX-129

GO
fish

the overlook press
woodstock · new york

First published in 1995 by
The Overlook Press
Lewis Hollow Road
Woodstock, New York 12498

Available on video from Evergreen Entertainment and Samuel Goldwyn Home Entertainment.
For more information, write to:
   Evergreen Entertainment
   P.O. Box 4535
   Pacoima, CA 91333

Copyright © 1995 Guinevere Turner and Rose Troche
Foreword © 1995 Lea DeLaria

All Rights Reserved. No part of this publication may be reproduced or transmitted in any form by any
means, electronic or mechanical, including photography, recording, or any information storage and
retrieval system now known or to be invented without permission in writing from the publisher, except by
a reviewer who wishes to quote brief passages in connection with a review written for inclusion in a magazine, newspaper, or broadcast.

Library of Congress Cataloging-in-Publication Data

Turner, Guinevere.
   Go Fish / Guinevere Turner, Rose Troche; foreword by Lea Delaria
   p. cm.
1. Go Fish (Motion Picture) I. Troche, Rose. II. Title.
PN1997.G5573T87 1995
791.43'72–dc20
94-47245
CIP
ISBN: 0-87951-591-0

First Edition

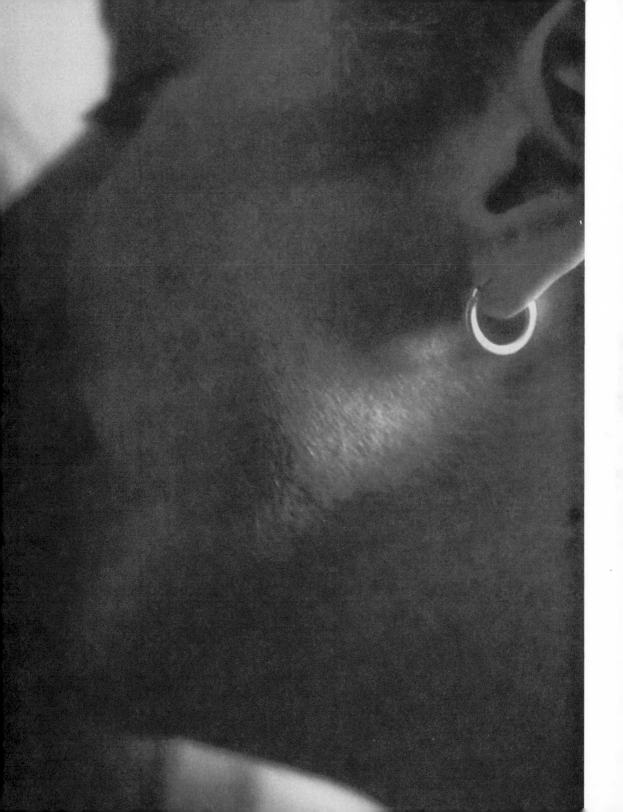

foreword

When I was just a spit of a dyke about yea high, everything was a secret. You see, I was raised in a typically American momdadbudandsis dysfunctional fashion. I recognized "unique" qualities within myself. For example, in my neighborhood, "Star Trek" was the pretend game of choice. I fought the boys to be Captain Kirk . . . and won. It was obvious what made me "unique." I was different. Barbie dolls were to be stripped then decapitated in some sort of bizarre pre-adolescent S&M ritual. My difference was apparent. Everyone saw. My family noticed. My friends noticed. Yes, even the nuns who taught me knew I was not like the other little girls, for nuns never miss a damn thing, trust me. Yet, with all this blatant observing going on, no one ever said a word to me. That would be telling. It was up to me to me to discover who and what I was. So, like everyone in my generation who was trapped in the Midwest, I got my information from the movies.

I remember my first exposure to lesbianism in film. The movie, *Rachel, Rachel,* was directed by Paul Newman and starred Joanne Woodward. The sight of terrified Joanne Woodward, racing from the shadow of the tree where Estelle Parsons has attempted to kiss her, delayed my coming out process by a good eight months.
I saw, in order, *The Children's Hour, The Killing of Sister George, Rebecca, No Exit, Julia* and *Prisoner of Cell Block H* . It's a wonder I am able to look into a vagina at all.

Time passes. I am older. I still consider myself "unique" in that gestalt Italian sort of way. I am a total dyke; after all, you are what you eat. We lesbians have our own movies now. I've seen them all. I march proudly to festivals, anxious to cross the threshold and drown myself in an ocean of pro-lesbian filmmaking. Boy, have I seen a lot of crap.

There has been a seemingly endless procession of disappointing films which we all raced to view simply due to their gay-girl content. There are some exceptions: *I've Heard The Mermaid Singing, Oranges Are Not The Only Fruit* and *Joan D"Arc of Outer Mongolia* come to mind. All three are enormously entertaining. All three are non-American. And finally, all three are far-fetched fantastical stories that have little or nothing to do with me, my life, or who I am.

Some of this must have clicked with Rose Troche and Guinevere Turner, for they made *Go Fish* a sobering, humorous and strikingly realistic slice of survival in Chicago's dyke ghetto. This is Max and Ely's universe, my universe. A galaxy filled with process, dating and sex; sex and queer arts; sex and vegetarianism, radical feminism, racism, sleeping with men, monogamy, penetration, and safe sex (not dental dams but cutting your nails!). Here are all the intricacies which combine to make up the world in which I live and love. In short, this movie rings true.

sis: "mom, dad's passed out from a drug overdose."

mom: "he's just sleeping, dear, and pick up your socks."

lea delaria, los angeles, 1995

rose troche

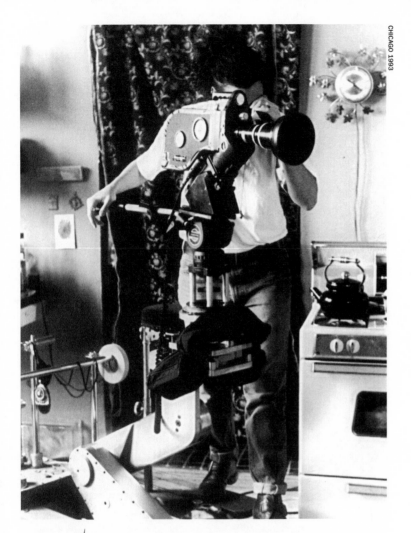

We have been asked thousands of times how *Go Fish* began. At this point, I am pretty convinced we have reconstructed the history of the project. The story goes something like this: Guin and I started in August of 1991, this was the talking stage. At this point we were still involved in Act Up Chicago, which provided Guin and me the first opportunities to work together. We did several performance pieces and a benefit together so we felt we had a pretty good idea of what it was like to work together. Wrong. This memory is fact; nothing we had ever done together would prepare us to embark upon the thing that is now *Go Fish*.

We thought about what we wanted to represent in a lesbian film. The diversity of the community. Back then we thought there was indeed a lesbian community, and it was that community to which we wanted to give *Go Fish*. Not only for them, but for us. Guin and I spoke

finally we concluded, we will write a script that depicts a lesbian community, with women who are twenty some- thing with sketchy careers, and girlfriends who call in sick.

ELY & MAX WAS THE ORIGINAL TITLE OF *GO FISH*.

of the things we felt were missing from lesbian images we had run across, whether in film, video or photography, and those things which were present that we wanted to restate. Finally, we concluded, we will write a script that depicts a lesbian community, with women who are twentysomething with sketchy careers and girlfriends who call in sick. We also wanted to have our characters have a sense of humor, that fluctuated between taking themselves too seriously to not at all. We spoke at length about the kind of situations we wanted to represent. Romance, yes. Sex, yes, yes.

In November of 1991, we shot the first bit of film that was at that point called *Ely and Max*. It was documentary footage. Footage that would later be dropped from the film. But at the time it served the pur- pose of validating the beginnings of a feature length film. We were down right excited. We had gone to clubs and functions passing out invitations that asked any woman in our path to be a part of an open shoot for a new and exciting lesbian movie. Guin and I came up with the questions.

What do you call yourself, in regard to your sexuality? What do you find attractive in a woman? What is sexy to you? Will you give us money to make this film? If not, will you work on this film? Woe was us to the people who answered negatively to all of the above.

When we saw our first reels of *Ely and Max* we were thrilled, they were far too dark with no beautiful back light or for that matter beautiful anything, but they were ours. After several of these open shoots we realized the film would be more expensive than anticipated.

Prior to this point we had not hit anyone up for money, not because we didn't plan to, but simply because we hadn't gotten around to it. So we began the fund raising process or the frustrating process as I like to call it. I don't exactly know what we were thinking when we thought our fellow sisters would give money to this worthy project. Unfortunately, the well was dry. As a bone. As usual. We asked ourselves, where are our rich lesbian friends, and why have they forsaken us? That's when we realized, we knew no rich lesbians, as a matter of fact isn't that an oxymoron? Aren't we all social workers, teachers, terminal students, slackers and such and such? My conclusion to these questions was, you're darn tootin' we are. After this epiphany, Guin and I decided to take the old fashioned route and have a benefit, after all we were familiar with this process. The beer was free, the women were loose, what more could you ask for? Personally, I could have asked for more money. We made under $900 on the event. More important we learned a valuable lesson — to save our energy on the task ahead. We realized we could burn out on benefits before we got anything on celluloid.

There was one more thing that took me a moment to recognize — that I could not do everything myself. If I wanted to make a feature film I had to learn how to be that kind of director. I had to learn how delegate responsibility. My background had been in short experimental films. I would conceptualize, shoot, edit and deliver all on my own. It was quite a shift to move into the format of feature length narrative where it is much more of a collective process. I had to admit to myself there are people out there who know how to light better, shoot better, the whole nine yards. In other words I recognized I needed a crew.

In the spring of 1992 I was asked to be in a program, "Who's Zooming Who? Lesbians on Tape." This was part of a series called "In Through the Out Door."I was thrilled to be in the show, it gave me a personal deadline to have a work-in-progress screening of *Ely and Max.*

Guin and I spoke again about content. At this point there was no practical script, just a series of ideas for the narrative. I wanted to have something in the movie about relationships between mother and daughter, so I thought the first voice over of the film could deal with this. Guin and I both took a stab at writing this voice-over, as a matter of fact, that is the last stab I ever took at writing a voice-over; It was

CHICAGO 1993

CHICAGO 1993

Guin who would ultimately come up with the voice-over that would become the wedding sequence, and to this day, my favorite scene in *Go Fish*.

It was also around this time Guin and I were introduced to a quiet, intense woman named Ann Rossetti. Ann was about to graduate from Columbia College with a degree in cinematography. Perfect. Ann gave *Ely and Max* the fresh perspective and drive it needed to keep moving. She was enthusiastic and I was beside myself with our good fortune. After all who else would have given her all to a project that, although we didn't know it at the time, would take almost two more years to complete.

We were ready for action. We had a fabulous voice-over, a skilled DP, a cheap dolly and a concept. Again we called upon our friends to help. Again they were there for us. Although I don't think I let them know up front they would not only have to put a wedding dress on — they would also have to take it off.

We shot the wedding sequence in one day, in a dusty loft in Wicker Park, Chicago. I don't think anything can compare to seeing that footage. It looked just like a real movie. I transferred the footage to video along with the documentary footage we shot late in 1991. We had also shot some exteriors, that were to be used as transitional elements between the documentary, experimental and narrative portions. Now all I had to figure out was how to put it together. The screening was sched- uled for May 30, 1992, the day I would turn twenty-eight, the day I would be accused of trying to steal Elvis, but that's a whole other story. Hours before the screening I was still online editing. This is what you call "pulling a Troche." That is, you do it and keep doing till the clock runs out, or someone rips it out of your hands. With the help and patience of Henrique Cirne Lama, who guided me through that first bout with editing, we managed to get done, with enough time to race the tape into the gallery, take a seat and watch for the first time *Ely and Max*: a work in progress. The screening went very well. Response from the audience was overwhelmingly positive. For myself, it was the first time I had screened several works as a body before an audience, and it served to validate my position as a filmmaker in an environment out- side of school. I felt as though I would be able to approach people for financial help and not have them think I was using the money to buy a Maserati.

The same evening of that screening a friend approached me and asked if I had an assistant director. Of course...I don't, I replied. He suggested a woman by the name of Wendy Quinn, and gave me her number. I called and she showed up. I was vaguely familiar with Ms. Quinn through her performances as Liz Taylor. Chicago is a very multi conceptual place. Meeting Wendy was another burst of adrenaline to the project. Here was a woman with experience, a woman who could tell a room full of people who were working for free, they had two minutes to eat lunch and thirty seconds to set up for the next shot. It's a good thing we weren't shooting under water. She was organized, firm and calm — all the makings of a perfect AC.

Gaily we moved forward. Oh for the determination of young naive ambition. By this time we had a working script, which was forever being revised, even on the days we shot.

Now we needed a cast. Oh my kingdom for a cast, I cried into my beer. I already knew V.S. Brodie and Guin Turner would play the roles of *Ely and Max* respectively, but what about the rest of them?

T. Wendy McMillan, generous soul that she is, showed up at one of our open documentary shoots. I saw her on film and thought she had a good presence. After discussing it with Guin, we decided to offer her the part of Kia, a thirtysomething women's studies teacher who has a blazer fetish and a girlfriend named Evy. She said yes, we said thank you.

Next, who would play the infamous role of Daria, the greasy ho, woman's woman? I don't know — it sounded like a good part to me.

It so happens Guin and I frequented a restaurant called Leo's Lunchroom, again in Wicker Park, Chicago. At this humble little restaurant worked a woman named Anastasia Sharp. At that time we didn't know her name, we only knew she hung out around the neighborhood. The biggest question was, Who did she hang out with? Wicker Park was mainly a Latino area with artists, gays and lesbians moving in, as well as unwelcome yuppies who were attracted by the low real estate costs. Now all we needed to determine was what category Anastasia fit in. Hmm, let me see? At the time Guin and I were elbowing each other, in a you ask her, no, you ask her way, Anastasia was bald and servin' up some pork chop. Hello to the clueless ones, proper hair cut and occupation, knock knock. Well at least someone was home. I believe it was Guin who finally got up enough nerve to ask Anastasia if she was interested in being in the movie. You have to understand to ask someone if they were interested was to basically ask them if they were a dyke. And believe it or not some people might have been a tiny bit offended because after all, we all know it is a shameful and degrading thing to be. Our luck, she was indeed shameful and degraded, she said yes to our offer. Hey, this is not half bad.

Only one more.

You may ask, why didn't we have a casting call? A casting couch, for that matter. Well, here it is, in a couple of nut shells. First, *Go Fish* was lower than low budget. I didn't even feel like I had the authority to have a casting call. The people who participated in the movie did so because they had a entirely different motivation. That was, to see lesbian images, real lesbian images, portrayed on a big or even tiny screen. Visibility was one of the prime considerations of the project. Second, the material was such that a nonprofessional in most cases was most familiar with it, if she was a lesbian who came from the same area. It was a slice of Wicker Park dyke life. And indeed the entire cast and most of the crew took up habitation in this now infamous neighborhood. Last, I have to admit I didn't know if we could ever ultimately pull it off and I did not want to risk the time it would take to finish when the careers of people who were dead serious about their acting were at stake. So it was just a heck of a lot easier to get people to work on the

you may ask, why didn't we have a casting call. a casting couch, for that matter.

SATURDAY, JANUARY 25

• WE NEED LESBIANS •

FOR AN OPEN SHOOT

BE IN ELY & MAX

NOON TO SEVEN BOTH DAYS
(COME ON EITHER DAY)
2-4 HOUR COMMITMENT

1 9 4 9   W .   C R Y S T A L ,   # 3

SUNDAY, JANUARY 26

EQUIPMENT USE AGREEMENT

Agreement dated ___Dec. 4 72___ , between

___Rosemarie Reum___ , hereinafter known as

USER and Edward T. McDougal, 350 Adams Avenue, Glencoe, Illinois 60022, 312-

835-5333, hereinafter known as OWNER.

For the consideration of ___$250.00___ , OWNER

hereby loans the following equipment to USER.

___2 Baby's - Fresnel___

___1 Arri Kit with stands___

___7 C-stands w/ 1 arm + head each___

___11 Sand Bags___

___1 18x24 Flag___

___1 24x36 Flag___

___1 18x24 silk___

___1 24x36 silk___

---

it was just a heck of a lot easier to get people to work on the movie, who were motivated by more than shallow extrinsic goals, like money, fame and fortune.

movie, who were motivated by more than shallow extrinsic goals, like money, fame and fortune.

We were all ready setting up the production schedule and getting ready to move ahead while we searched for the final character, Evy. It was important for me to cast a woman who was Puerto Rican in the role and one who could also speak Spanish and one who also was a lesbian and one who also would give an open ended commitment to the project, through thick and thin. No big thing, right?

Into the night I went. Evy, where for art thou, Evy? Well, she was in a club. There she was, a vision, standing with a friend, in one of those clubs that is only a woman's club when the moon is full and the tide is high. Well at least it answered one question. I handed her a flyer to our benefit and asked her to please come, it's important, this is a moment in history, a turning point for lesbians everywhere, it's only five bucks. She came to the benefit, her name, Migdalia Melendez, hmm, Mel-en-dez. Well that answered any question about my other requirement. Now was she available? It turns out, Migdalia was interested in being in the movie, but, she had three jobs in addition to being a student at the Art Institute of Chicago. Aie yie yie, que lastima. Well do you think you could do it anyway? By this time I had become a bit more bold. She said yes, and that is how a group of women ended up being caretakers for a little girl named Tory. One of Migdalia's job was being a nanny, and this was the one job she could do while we shot. So while Migdalia was on camera, there were about three or four other women in the next room trying distract Tory enough to not notice Migdalia was gone. Let me tell you it was quite a sight, these women, who for the most part, did not give a thought to parenting, playing with this small child. Look at the shiny Zippo, ooh fire, yes, those are O B tampons, they're the best, you can just keep that for later.

CHICAGO 1993

It was June of 1992 when we started shooting the narrative portions of *Go Fish*. The equipment was coming from the University of Illinois, the Art Institute of Chicago, Northwestern University, Post Effects and Columbia College, and honey, it wasn't flying in on its own, I had to pick it up from all those places. A process which took several hours. I made a deal with my employer (or maybe I just said I was going on break), to leave work early on Fridays in order to make my pick ups. I left work at 3 p.m. and call time was at 6 p.m. I'm sure to this day Post Effects has the University of Illinois extension cord and Columbia College has a scrim from the Art Institute. None the less we had equipment, could shoot. The beginnings of production were exciting but difficult. Guin and I were wearing so many hats as a result of a lack of continuity in the people who production assisted or coordinated production. I had a certain possessiveness around the project that did not allow others to enter the process with full responsibility. Looking back on this, I see it as a kind of first feature syndrome, I wanted to own all aspects of the film making process and that I did, but definitely at a price.

During the beginning of production, a man named Art Stone, no relation to Oliver, was working as the lighting director. Art was a graduate student of film at the Art Institute, a school that champions experimental film making. I wanted to work with the notion that a simple, almost comedic, narrative feature could still be experimental, so I thought Art was a welcome addition to the crew. Ann Rossetti on the other hand was from the other school of film making, Columbia College that is, which strives for a more Hollywood approach. Things at Columbia are taught by the book and its students tend to be technically proficient in the craft of film making. Ann and Art were required to work closely together, of course, one was lighting and the other shooting. Unfortunately the two didn't get along and the balance I was hoping we would strike between the two different philosophies of film making only resulted in a stalemate. I was constantly asked to speak privately with Ann and then with Art. I simply could not create peace between the two, and it was beginning to show in the rushes.

The problem I was experiencing, which I'm sure many in no-budget film making have, is when friends give you their time for free, how do you tell them to get it together and be professional. Or, how do you tell them you think production would go more smoothly without them. My loyalties were divided, I did nothing and the situation esca-

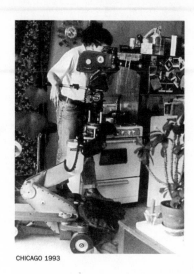

CHICAGO 1993

at the time guin and i were sinking every extra penny into production and cocktails (for medicinal purposes).

lated, until that dreaded day in December 1992. We were shooting the trial scene and the classroom scene all in one day. Ambitious? No. Crazy? Yes. It was an 18-hour shoot, with only one meal, people were mad. I was fairly clueless in my own world, concentrating and living on directing alone. The following day Art called me and quit. Actually he not only quit, he also told me what he thought about me and my rinky dink movie. He felt used, he felt as though I always agreed with Ann, he felt as though I took advantage of all those around me, I think abuse was the word he used. I hung up with Art and received a second call from a woman named Elspeth kydd. Elspeth was also a key crew person, who had dedicated an intense amount of time to *Go Fish*. She also quit, saying she had been pushed to her limit. I took their words to heart and canceled the remaining weeks of production, opting instead to wait for money and emotional repair. In other words, I cracked. I called Guin to tell her I cracked and I was canceling production for the moment. To this day I am not sure she understood I cracked, period.

My inability to move on at that moment created a predicament. We had already had a stop-and-start production period. People were starting to lose faith over the fruition of the project and now I was only complicating matters by falling apart. One must understand that Guin and I were looked upon to be optimistic at all times to give the project profundity. This was personally draining and if it weren't for Guin's strength and her refusal to crack, the project might never have gotten done.

I think I should say that I am not a weak woman. Maybe I will backtrack and describe some of the trials and tribulations this little movie put us through.

For the summer of 1992 we shot on the weekends — not every weekend, mind you. Sometimes we didn't have the money. The money was always just a couple of hundred dollars, but none the less, occasionally we did not have it, usually when rent was due. At the time Guin and I were sinking every extra penny into production and cocktails (for medicinal purposes). She worked as a topless dancer at a local strip joint, actually this is where we met. I got off work at the construction site, my fork lift busted a nut, so I was free, and decided to go see a little giggle, if you know what I mean. There she was. To this day I don't know if that was a twinkle in her eye when she winked at me or the disco ball reflecting light off her sequined g-string, whatever it was, I was hooked. I poured the rest of my Old Milwaukee into my hard hat and toasted the lady. He he, just kidding. Guin worked at a joint called Bricker and Associates, the kind of place that strips you of your identity, not your clothes, but heck it paid well. Unlike my job at the University library, stop laughing. I had a good time between those dark dusty shelves. My only fear was that I would start to become librarian like, bespectacled, head in the card catalog, brown bag lunch, 15 minute breaks, socially awkward when it came to talking about anything not related to the Dewey decimal system and my butt getting wider and wider as the years dragged on. Oh the nightmares I had!

Anyhow, there we were between these exciting careers trying

20

to make a movie. Driven in part by the dread of getting trapped in the mediocrity of our not quite white-collar existence.

The phone was off the hook continually as we called everyone we knew to come and help with the film. The crew was constantly shifting, we would make about twenty calls and get about two confirmations. So I never knew how many people were actually going to show up at any given shoot. To this day I have the utmost appreciation for those who worked on Go Fish continuously. It was hard work, long hours, not enough food, let alone a peanut M&M floating around. On several occasions we had fewer than five people working, these were the times when it was almost impossible to be free enough to direct, there were too many other things to attend to. One such occasion occurred when Ann Rossetti sprained her ankle while stepping off a curb in heels. See what happens when you put a dyke in a dress? Ann called and informed me of her physical limitation. Admittedly I was not very sympathetic, I was so caught up with the reality that I had no one to shoot at the weekend. I called a friend who recommended a DP, a professional at that. I called her and she agreed to meet, wow was I intimidated. The nice thing about Go Fish is the majority of us were "first timers," but virgins, this woman had been around the block, she was a regular Mac Daddy. I got my notes together and we talked, she said she would shoot for us. I quickly jotted down the long list of equipment she required. Equipment? I thought, can't ya just shoot with the three lights we got? You don't really need that dolly, do you? Mais oui, she sure did if she was gonna shoot for us and I sure did want her to do that. So Guin and I made a pact with our friend the devil and sold our souls in a two for one deal and got enough money to rent the additional costly material. There I was Friday afternoon. Load it up boys, sure the check's good, insurance, wha? Screech, I was burnin' rubber. When I got home and checked the answering machine there was a message informing me that my new DP friend would not be joining me this weekend, or any other for that matter, she had another commitment (probably paying, and I couldn't compete with that).

There I was — a van full of equipment and still no one to shoot. It was a martyr's wet dream. That's okay, I can do this by myself. No. Really, don't touch anything, it's good this way.

So, there I was trying to shoot the goddamn movie myself, cursing the heavens, the earth and all its low life inhabitants, myself being the only worthy one exempted. There are actually a number of film makers who write, direct, shoot and edit. My opinion is, it's a little too much to chew. I originally wanted to act in Go Fish as well, but I firmly believed I needed as much space as possible to direct and I didn't think I could do that in front of the camera or behind the lens.

So, as I said, there I was trying to shoot. Everything was set up, I was about to call action when the cavalry came. Thank God. Ann showed up, ace bandage around her ankle, goofy smile on her face, as she laughed at me trying to shoot, with a crew the size of a pea in a pod. Then get your ass back here, was all I could think. Pretty please. Once again Ann came through and saved my butt. Thanks, Ann.

GERMANY 1994

THE SAMUEL GOLDWYN COMPANY
invite you to meet
ROSE TROCHE
the director of

GO
fish

Official selection
Panorama Special 1994

at a cocktail reception at
Connection Bistro, Martin Luther Strasse 19,
1000 Berlin 30
on Monday 14th of February at 6.30 - 8.00 p.m

GO FISH will be screening at the following times

Monday 14th February at 11.30pm at Atelier am Zoo
Tuesday 15th February at 11.30pm at Filmpalast
Wednesday 16th February at 3.30pm at Filmpalast

strictly non-transferable
R.S.V.P. Caroline Henshaw
tel. (Berlin) 210 070   admit one
tel. (London) 071 486 5105   no admittance without invitation

GEN. ADM.

SEC.   ROW   SEAT

38

ADMIT ONE THIS DATE

MAY 12 1994

NY LESBIAN
AND GAY
FILM FESTIVAL
PRESENTS
GO FISH
OPENING NIGHT
BENEFIT
VILLAGE
EAST THEATER
181 2ND AVE
THU 8:00 PM

NO REFUNDS   PRICE   NO EXCHANGES

$20.00

SEC.   ROW   SEAT

38

GEN. ADM.

MAY 12 1994
THU 8:00 PM
$20.00
OPENING NIGHT
BENEFIT

We were back on track, shooting away. The crew still varied in size, shape and commitment level. The fluctuations were not so hard to handle. Although the lack of punctuality was. We would have call time at 9 a.m. on a Saturday morning and one could expect that by 11 a.m. the crew would finally be there, usually hung over, needing about 15 cups of coffee and 12 trips to the bathroom before we could really start. I guess I can't blame them, lord knows production has been the only thing I have been consistently on time for in my life.

Then the fateful day came when Wendy Quinn, the wonder AC, went from my right hand to my left foot. We were shooting the bookstore scene that day and after we were scheduled to shoot exteriors before we lost the sun. The scene went smoothly, we were on limited time, having to finish the scene before the store opened at 1 p.m. We had it in the can and were getting ready to move on when Wendy pulled me aside and said she couldn't work the remainder of the day. OK, no problem. So I'll see you tomorrow, right? As it turns out I wouldn't see her again until months later, Wendy got another job and I got an ulcer. While I wondered what I would do without Wendy and her calm determined manner on the set, Ann informed me she thought there was a problem with the magazine, causing all our footage to be fucked. I said, What!? No. No. Gimme that, I ripped the mag out of her hands and went into the bathroom, where it was dark (this was the weekend someone forgot to bring the changing bag). I blindly felt the roll of shot footage and it seemed just fine. What a relief. I came out of the bathroom in time to see Wendy leaving. Bye now. Come back soon. Sniffle. Ann was sitting on the couch of the bookstore with another magazine on her lap. I informed her the footage was fine and that I was relieved. She was too, so relieved she opened up the magazine that was on her lap, exposing all the footage we had shot the day before. Oopsie. This was the day I cried in the closet. Not because I'm a dirty homosexual, but because I obviously had a dirty soul because this was some bad karma coming to haunt me.

As if this was not enough, I have another horror story. The story of the day the last bit of our money disappeared. That's right, it got legs and ran away. I think that is the question I screamed to Guin when she informed me the money was gone. It was only $125, but it was all we had. It was the money that would get us through the next two days of shooting, the money that would buy food for the crew, the money that would buy me aspirins for my headache. We were shooting the Daria at work scene in a local bar in Wicker Park at a bar Guin and I frequented quite often, the Gold Star. They were kind enough to let us shoot with only a moments warning, and as a sunny summer afternoon will be in the Gold Star, there were customers. Crusty customers. Guin was holding our money in her day timer, which she placed on the bar. Well let's make a long story short shall we. About an hour later the day timer was there but not the money and I was back in the closet.

It's funny how everyone who makes a low or no budget feature has horror stories, that's just the nature of the beast. It takes money to make a film, but fortunately not that much. There are many times

that I think Guin and I had a lucky star shining on us. You just need to look at who we had the opportunity to work with. Christine Vachon, Tom Kalin, John Pierson and the Samuel Goldwyn Company. We were able to travel the world. I must say that in 1991, the year I got my degree and the year we started *Go Fish* if someone told me I would have the world premiere of my first feature screen at the Sundance Film Festival and sell to a major distributor the following day, I would have said you're drunk, because God knows it probably would have been Guin Turner saying those things, while sitting in a stool next to me at the Gold Star. God bless her beating hopeful heart.

rose troche, nyc, 1995

guinevere turner

W hen you tell a story over and over again the story changes, solidifies, and becomes increasingly removed from the actual event. If you tell a story over and over to the press, and you see your story in print and notice what they left out of what you told them, you slowly change the story into what you think the press will print. Or change the way you say it to get into print. So writing about the experience of making *Go Fish* and being made by *Go Fish* is a challenging task. If I had a dime for every time *Go Fish* put me in a situation that made me say "How the hell did I end up here?", I'd have about twenty bucks. So I'm just going to tell some of those stories, because they're funny and, to be honest, I'm not real-ly sure how we made *Go Fish*.

It was June of 1994 and Rose and I were in L.A. promoting the movie. "Promoting the movie" means doing 10-15 interviews a day, even during lunch, and answering the same questions over and over. "Why did you make it in Black and White?" "So, were those all of your friends?" (Like my friends are that nice to each other in real life). "How

i was like yeah sure whatever let's do it and get out of creepy l.a. but now i wonder... what was the significance of photographing us in front of a huge donut? was it some comparison of the female body to a donut, and if so, should we be insulted? i don't particularly identify with donuts.

PHOTO BY CHRIS BUCK, LOS ANGELES 1994

much of that was improvised?" (Half of one scene. The question always offended me for some reason. I guess because it implied that we were just a bunch of gals goofing around with some camera equipment.) Anyway Rose and I would get totally delirious and hysterical by the end of a day like that and smoke way too many cigarettes and have headaches and be ready for a cocktail.

In L.A., the man assigned to take care of us and shuffle us around was Chip, a well-meaning queen with the gift of gab. When he wasn't telling us about his life or telling us we couldn't smoke for TV interviews (I thought it would be cool to be seen on E! smoking but Chip wasn't having it), he would sing the song that was originally at the end of *Go Fish*, which we couldn't get the rights to. It was called "I Need Your Love" by a British group called N.R.G. Needless to say, it was the perfect song—it was a big fat bummer that we couldn't use it, and to have someone singing it to us all day was a little rough.

Finally, it was 5:00 and Chip said all we had to do was one photo session for the *Independent* in England, and then we would go to the airport and fly to Seattle? San Fran? I don't remember. So the photographer, Chris Buck, wants to take us somewhere in this rented red convertible (whatever that big swanky boulevard is in L.A. with all of the palm trees) and it ends up that he wants me to stand on the back of the car while Chip slowly drives it. Rose was sitting at my feet, also up on the back of the car. I occasionally had to grab her head for balance. This fiasco continued for about an hour, and I was really worked by the end of it, Chip chattering on and on and the photographer wanting Rose and me to kiss. (We look at each other and point "Her? You want me to kiss her?" and then bust out laughing.) Suddenly the photographer has an inspiration—there's some huge donut on the L.A. freeway and *that's* the perfect place to photograph us. At the time I was like yeah sure whatever let's do it and get out of creepy L.A., but now I wonder—what was the significance of photographing us in front of a huge donut? Was it some comparison of the female body to a donut, and if so, should we be insulted? I don't particularly identify with donuts. I guess I'll never know. So all of a sudden Chip becomes vaguely hysterical—he was like a wacky wind-up toy having its last eerily sped-up effort before it collapses in the corner. He talks to the driver who's taking us to the airport and explains about the donut and says the photographer will show you where and don't let these girls miss their plane and something about 20 minutes and for us to run upstairs and pack and then he disappeared forever and I never saw him again. Rose and I go running upstairs and I dash into my room and pack furiously, having anxiety abut missing our plane, thinking it was a situation like this that made me leave all of my best underwear in a drawer in a hotel room in London. In five minutes I am knocking on Rose's door, suitcase in hand, ready to go. She says, "Come in" and she's lying on her bed, drinking a beer, watching cartoons, utterly unpacked and relaxed. I'm not lying.

PHOTO BY CHRIS BUCK, LOS ANGELES 1994

Rose Troche will be late for her own funeral. In fact I have been late for a funeral with Rose, but it was partially my fault. She also doesn't respond well to hysteria, which is something I can produce in the form of a continuous 10 minute sentence at the drop of a hat. So I tried calmly to tell her that we really REALLY had to get our asses down to the lobby in five minutes or we were screwed and Chip was history so I don't know what we would've done if we missed our plane. I forget what her response was but I had to leave the room while she packed because otherwise we would've gotten into a fight and I wanted to look happy in front of that donut. We stood in front of the donut, or more nearly we had to stand on an island in the middle of an expressway to appear like we were standing in front of the donut, we got to the airport, I lost my plane ticket and we got into a huge fight. ("Why were you so nice to her? She's not just gonna *give* you another ticket?" "Just get on the stupid plane and I'll deal with this myself." "Are you sure you looked in the bathroom?" "No, Rose, I'm incapable of looking for a plane ticket in a bathroom.") Anyway it was in the bathroom (Rose found it, but it wasn't that I didn't see it, it was that I was looking in the wrong bathroom) and we made the plane and got out of L.A. and that's the end of the story.

Right after the Samuel Goldwyn Company bought *Go Fish* they slapped together an image for a full page ad in *Variety* in time for the American Film Market, which is where people come from all over the world te arms and stout body they fused onto me. The only other person on the poster was a woman who's in the movie for about 15 seconds and looks really straight. Together we looked like a mother and daughter, I triumphant after winning a very special race, she ever-sup-

שמחים להזמינכם
להקרנה ומסיבת גג פרועה לסרט:

Go Fish

בנוכחות:
הבמאית רוז טרוש וכוכבת הסרט גווין טרנר

ההקרנה תתקיים בבתי קולנוע לב
יום חמישי 7.7.94 בשעה 20.00
מסיבה על גג דיזנגוף סנטר
מיד בתום ההקרנה

הזמנה זוגית אישית

SAMUEL GOLDWYN COMPANY 1994
ISRAEL PROMOTIONAL FLYER
HEAD BY GUINEVERE TURNER, LESBIAN
BODY BY FEMALE, UNKNOWN SEXUAL ORIENTATION

we laughed our asses off for about an hour, just at the image of my head fused onto someone else's body

portive. The tag line read "Sex is important. So is friendship, romance and laundry." For whom, one might ask, for whom are these things important? So we laughed our asses off for about an hour, just at the image of my head fused onto someone else's body in a magazine, (we can be simple like that sometimes) and the we said "Oh fuck." We worked on it with them, liking "The girl is out there" much better as a tag line because while it still didn't make the subject and content of the movie clear, (Shhh . . . they'll figure it out when they get there), it did imply that perhaps it was a movie about a female serial killer, which would also be cool.

Maybe I should start from the beginning. I guess if you think about it, *Go Fish* was actually able to be at a theater near you because of certain people we met along the way. The first time I really felt like "Holy shit, we're really going to movie" was after we met Ann T. Rossetti, out cinematographer. We met Ann, oddly enough on Christmas Eve, 1991, and ended up having Christmas dinner with her. She didn't say much (she was with our friend T. Wendy McMillan, who plays Kia) but I do remember well the first time she mumbled something about shooting movies. She continued to be a big one for mumbling, but we ended up asking her to shoot with us one day (One of Rose's harebrained schemes—I had written a voice-over about the security of heterosexual marriage and Rose wanted to film me and others in a wedding dress. "Oh God Rose, that's so *literal*," I whined, but it turned out to be one of our favorite scenes in the movie). Ann and Rose worked beautifully together that day (I speculate now that it's because Ann got to see the tits of several strangers) and we all went out afterwards and felt elated. Ann was amazingly committed to be ours, for as long as it took, with no pay or promise of pay. And I really don't know why, because to this day I don't think she's read the script of *Go Fish*. Maybe it was that psychotically determined/foolish look that Rose and I had in our eyes when we talked seriously about making a movie for $7,000.

Then there was meeting Christine Vachon. It was early fall of 1992, we had already shot over half the movie, ruined everyone's summer, borrowed everyone's money, done untold damage to everyone's apartments that we shot in, and we were totally out of money scam options. Rose called a bunch of people, one of whom was Christine Vachon in New York. At the time, Christine was getting a lot of hype around *Swoon*, Tom Kalin's feature (and Tom could be seen gracing the pages of *Out* magazine in glamorous make up). She had already produced Todd Haynes's *Poison*, which also got a lot of media attention, and "New Queer Cinema" had allegedly been born. (Apparently, it was a boy.) When Rose called her, Christine said "Send me a tape and a script," which gave us much hope at the time, although we now know that tapes and scripts pile up and collect dust not only in Christine's office but in the office or home of any person who's in the position to produce or financially back a movie. We sent our script with some parts missing (like how it ends) and a 15 minute tape of some scenes we had shot that we transferred to video and edited, and a heartfelt letter

28 ⌗

about how "the world needs more lesbian films." She called the next day to say she wanted to take the project on.

We felt like two queens of France as we drove to New York to meet her. We stood outside the door of her office going "You open it. No, you open it." It should be noted here that I thought behind the door would be a big marble reception area and that Christine would fully be in her office in a swivelly leather chair, slick, impatient and with finger-nail polish. I forget who opened the door, but there was a small two-room office full of stuff and people. There were two hip/grungy peo-ple sort of sprawled on the secondhand couch and several people on the phone, one of whom was Christine, in a modest but swivelly chair, with a baseball hat on, and several cups of coffee on her desk. It was my first lesson in "Just because you see someone in magazines a lot doesn't mean they have a lot of money." She took us to lunch and walked really fast and talked even faster and we were thrilled out of our minds that she believed in our movie. She told us she was forming a company with Tom Kalin called Kalin Vachon Productions and that together they were going to be our Executive Producers, which meant they would find us money to finish *Go Fish*.

She found us John Pierson. Movies that John has given com-pletion money to include *She's Gotta Have It*, *Roger and Me*, *Slacker*, and *Laws of Gravity*. I don't think I even knew that when Rose and I walked into John's Chicago hotel room with our little tape tucked under our arm. It was a Sunday morning in January, 1993, and it had been the usual Turner/Troche fiasco getting there. Just moments before Rose had been sweet-talking a cab driver into believing that really, someone was going to show up in another cab in a second with the money to pay her fare. I showed up moments later with the cash. We were slightly late and nervous as hell. A the front desk we hit a famil-iar impasse: "You call up." "No, you call." "I'm *always* the one." "Oh my God, just give me the fucking phone." We get up there and John was clearly getting rid of whoever had been pitching something to him before us. I think we apologized for being late and he said it was okay and that the people he was just talking to were dreaming if they thought he was going to be involved in whatever they were doing. Gulp. We pop in the tape and John flings himself onto the big bed like a schoolgirl, feet up in the air and hand on chin. We were sitting behind him, and we looked at each other with raised eyebrows like "I guess that's a good sign," and watched the tape. For me, the weirdest, most nerve-wracking part was watching the sex scene in this context, something I had already seen in its unedited form many times (now there's some funny stuff) and thought I was desensitized to. I was trying to be adult about it, but Rose and I both had to look away from the screen and make faces at each other. If someone had said to me a year before "In a year you'll be in a hotel room showing a man you've never met before a tape of yourself having sex with a woman and trying to get him to give you money," I would've been a little nervous about my future. But crap-py sound, poor video quality, unfinished script and all, he decided to do it.

CHICAGO 1993

🐟 29

PROMOTIONAL FLYER
JAPAN 1994

just because you see someone in magazines alot doesn't mean they have alot of money

We traveled the world and twelve U.S. cities with *Go Fish*. In Tel Aviv, *Go Fish* played in a mall with *Free Willy* and *Kalifornia*. In Barcelona they had a big, eerie hand painted version of the poster hanging outside the theater. In London we got a standing ovation. In Berlin we missed out flight home because Rose was making out with some fraulein on the stairs. I went to the Deauville Film Festival in France alone, and met a famous action star who shall remain nameless. He encouraged me to sit down, began talking, and eventually asked me if I wanted to come up to his room and have a drink. I declined politely, he insisted, I said "No, really, I . . . " and he promised a good time and finally I said "I'm a lesbian" and he said "I give really good head." Yum. In Jerusalem, Rose and I decided to take an afternoon stroll and enjoy the holiness of it all, and ended up walking for hours down a four lane highway, parched and laughing at the half-assed map that had led us here. We finally saw civilization in the form of a small grocery store, bought some water and were told that we were in Bethlehem of all places. We sat on a stoop in silence for a few minutes getting the dust out of our noses and rehydrating and Rose just said "Oh, little town" and our tacky clueless American laughter rattled down the dusty roads of the birthplace of Jesus.

On my birthday we were in Dallas, Texas, doing interviews all day and I was in a terrible mood. Our publicist, in charge of feeding us and shuttling us around was a bubbly Texas blonde. She picked us up from the airport in an insanely long white limousine, and you could tell it was just like the prom all over again for her. The best part was, you could tell she was kind of scared of us. When you meet someone and you realize that you are probably the only lesbian they think they've ever had to talk to, you realize that you have an advantage. At least if it's their job to talk to you. So we start talking about *Four Weddings and a Funeral*, and she's all dreamy about Hugh Grant. So one of us just says "He's gay, you know." I don't really have any idea about Hugh Grant's sexual preference; he just needed to be gay for us in this moment. Her face turned all twisty and she said "No, he's not." And we were deadpan, "No, really, everybody knows he's gay." She got really upset and looked like she was going to cry and finally said "Just because a guy is sensitive doesn't mean he has to be gay!" She was really flustered and changed the subject to Rose's eyebrow pierce. Rose is deliberately trying to freak her out by talking about nipple and genital piercing, and I gratuitously launch into a story about a friend of mine who's clit piercing got caught on her motorcycle while it was falling over, and the blood, screaming, etc. The publicist was really freaked out and we were pleased with ourselves. She dropped is off and took the white limo to a Salt 'N' Pepa concert, which she told us the next day was very "feminine" because they had "the men in cages." I think she meant feminist.

I'm just mad because my friend who produced *Clerks* had to deal with her when he was promoting in Texas and he told me that she said to him "Yeah, I met Rose and Guin. Rose is really nice. I think she's the one who's really a lesbian—that Guin flirts with men a lot."

JAPAN 1994

Whatever, babe.

But I digress. In December, 1994, we went to Tokyo with *Go Fish*. I had a lot of time for deep thoughts in Tokyo because I really couldn't wrap my mind around the Japanese language, even to identify a word here or there, so unless someone was directly addressing me I was left to my own devices. We were in this lesbian bar where they were having a *Go Fish* party. It was packed and frenzied and they treated us like celebrities. *Go Fish* was playing in a loop in one corner. I looked up at the screen, and there's me and Migdalia (Evy) sitting on the stairs and I got tears in my eyes. I thought about the day we shot that, March of 1993, in the stairwell of my apartment, ten or twelve of us jammed into this narrow space on a Sunday afternoon on the four millionth take and for what? None of us had any idea what it would become. A movie, hopefully, but that's about as far as we had thought about it. I was first wishing that all of the people who worked on it could see the strange, far-reaching life it now had, and thinking "Migdalia, you're on a big screen in a dyke bar in Tokyo. Weird, right?" and second, being amazed at the idea that the things you make can take you places. And a Japanese lesbian came up to me and said "I like your movie. It's really cute." That's what they said about it in Japan. "It's cute." "We are just three Japanese girls and we want to tell you that we don't know about politics and all that stuff but we think your movie is very cute." I was cute, Rose was cute, food was cute, phrases were cute. It was cute to be there and sad to leave and I guess it was monumental because it was one of our last trips with the movie and it was going on fully four years since *Go Fish* was a twinkle in mine and Rose's eyes.

Famous people I got to meet because of *Go Fish*? Matthew

we are just three japanese girls and we want to tell you that we don't know about politics and all that stuff but we think your movie is very cute.

🐟 31

go fish is a poor bet to keep you entertained unless youre (a) not just a gay woman, but militantly so, (b) a devotee of non-stop chatter, as opposed to action of any kind, and (c) convinced that the fullest expression of the coming-of-age of an oppressed minority lies in its ability to discuss sex ad nauseum...

Modine, who was one of the judges at the Sundance Film Festival where *Go Fish* had its world premiere. I met Eric Stoltz in a hotel lobby in Paris. He said "Hi, how are you?" Marlo Thomas presented us with the GLAAD Media Award that *Go Fish* won, and she was nice but I don't think she saw the movie. But Phil Donohue showed up and he shook our hands and said "Way to go, girls." Marisa Tomei sat next to me and said, "I loved your movie." She is even cuter in real life than in the movies. I met the fabulous and adorable Wilson Cruz from *My So Called Life*, the one who plays the gay kid. Somebody told me that Boy George loved the movie. The people at the Angelika Film Center where *Go Fish* showed in New York would tell me "Kim and Thurston from Sonic Youth saw it today" or "Sandra Bernard saw it." Which prompted a friend of mine to ask me "Do you think Madonna will see it?" If she did, she never called to talk about it. But 17-year old Tracey Thomas did, and she calls me from San Antonio occasionally to chat about life as an Asian lesbian in Texas, and once asked me a list of questions that she and her friends got together for me, including "Are you a cat person or a dog person?" "Do you think Elvis is still alive?" Dog. No. "Cool, thank you so much you probably think I'm a total geek." Not at all. "And if I can just say it again, me and my friends really loved your movie." I love that.

So I just want to thank some people. Christine Vachon, for being the first one to believe in us. Tom Kalin for taking care of our sorry butts all the time. John Pierson for giving us the money to finish, of course, but also for his love of good movies and getting them out into the world. All of the crazy Chicago gang who slaved on *Go Fish* with us. I know not where the dedication came from, but I am deeply grateful. V.S. Brodie especially, who not only acted, cooked, hauled equipment, ran errands between takes and pretended to have sex with me on film for the good of humanity, but who leant us both big chunks of change. I hope by the time you're reading this I don't still owe you any of it. To all the people who gave me money, a place to stay, a free cocktail and whatever else I needed during rougher times, thank you thank you. To the amazing people (all but two of them women) who own the companies in England, Ireland, Australia, Israel, Japan, Italy, France, and Spain that bought and showed *Go Fish* in theaters in those countries, , thank you for loving our movie and thank you for bringing us around the world.

Finally, I'd like to end with a quote from my favorite horrified review of *Go Fish*, from a New Orleans newspaper, titled "No Hook in Go Fish." ". . . *Go Fish* is a poor bet to keep you entertained unless you're (a) not just a gay woman, but militantly so, (b) a devotee of non-stop chatter, as opposed to action of any kind, and (c) convinced that the fullest expression of the coming-of-age of an oppressed minority lies in its ability to discuss sex *ad nauseum*..."

Don't you think that's funny?

guinevere turner, nyc, 1995

DATE: June 10, 1994

TO: All Concerned

FROM: Publicity

RE: GO FISH

Attached please find the following press clippings regarding GO FISH:

6/13	PEOPLE MAGAZINE/Leah Rosen	POSITIVE
6/17	ENTERTAINMENT WEEKLY/Lisa Schwarzbaum	POSITIVE
6/14	THE VILLAGE VOICE/J. Hoberman	POSITIVE
6/9	GANNETT SUBURBAN NEWSPAPERS/Marshal Fine	MIXED-POSITIVE
6/10	SIXTY SECOND PREVIEW/Jeff Craig	MIXED-NEGATIVE
7/94	VANITY FAIR MAGAZINE/Duncan Bock	INTERVIEW
6/94	INTERVIEW MAGAZINE/Henry Cabot Beck	MENTION
6/14	THE VILLAGE VOICE/Hoberman	ITEM
6/1	THE AQUARIAN WEEKLY/Prairie Miller	INTERVIEW
6/5	SAN FRANCISCO CHRONICLE/Dan Levy	INTERVIEW

5th Floor
Samuel Goldwyn, Jr.   Rose Troche
Meyer Gottlieb
Tom Rothman   Guin Turner
Norman Flicker
Ronna Wallace   Christine Vachon

4th Floor   Tom Kalin
Rich Bornstein
Dan Gelfand
Tricia Lambert
Sue Blackmore

3rd Floor
Eammon Bowles
Steve Bickel
Andrew Milner

Caroline Henshaw

GO fish

CREDITS

ISLET PRESENTS

A CAN I WATCH PICTURES PRODUCTION

IN ASSOCIATION WITH KVPI

PRODUCED BY ROSE TROCHE AND GUINEVERE TURNER

okay let's have a . . . make a list of women that you think are lesbians or that you know are lesbians through history and in the present time . . .

CLASSROOM

An African-American woman in her mid-thirties stands before an intimate classroom. She wears glasses and a blazer, which is her signature article of clothing. She is Kia, a teacher at a small college. She is teaching a women's studies class. She addresses her classroom.

KIA

Okay let's have a . . . make a list of women that you think are lesbians or that you know are lesbians through history and in the present time . . .

STUDENT #1

Eve

STUDENT #2

Eve who?

Laughter from the class and Kia, as she writes the names on the board.

STUDENT #3

Sappho?

STUDENT #4

Hannah Höch

STUDENT #5

Who is Hannah Höch?

STUDENT #6

Lily Tomlin

KIA

Lily Tomlin, okay—who else?

STUDENT #3

Dennis the Menace's next-door neighbor Margaret?

STUDENT #4

Whitney Houston?

STUDENT #1

Kristy McNichol?

STUDENT #4

Angela Davis

STUDENT #5

Mary Lou Retton.

STUDENT #3

(disbelief)

Mary Lou Retton?

EVERYONE

Virginia Woolf... Marilyn Quayle... Olivia Newton John... Chelsea Clinton

37

Kia races to write the names on the board. The class now on a roll, speeds ahead of her.

> KIA
>
> OK, you have to slow down . . .

> STUDENT #3
>
> What about Peppermint Patty?

> STUDENT #6
>
> Endora from "Bewitched?"

> STUDENT #3
>
> Agnes Moorehead

> STUDENT #4
>
> Agnes Moorehead?

> STUDENT #5
>
> The entire cast of "Roseanne"...

Entire class cracks up.

> KIA
>
> Except for Dan, right?

CREDIT WRITTEN BY GUINEVERE TURNER AND ROSE TROCHE

Dolly forward to see one of the students getting fed up with the current class activities. She throws her folder in front of her.

> STUDENT #7
>
> Excuse me, I have a question . . .

> KIA
>
> Yes?

STUDENT #7

Why . . . why are we even making this list? I mean, it's completely speculation.

KIA

That's a really good question. Throughout lesbian history there has been a serious lack of evidence that'll tell us what these women's lives were truly about. I mean lesbian lives and lesbian relationships—they barely exist on paper, and it is with that in mind and understanding the power of history . . .

CREDIT   EXECUTIVE PRODUCERS TOM KALIN   CHRISTINE VACHON

KIA

. . . That, we begin to want to change history.

CREDIT   GO FISH DIRECTED BY ROSE TROCHE

i have this great

fear that the

moment we were

supposed to meet

will be thwarted thwarted thwarted thwarted thwarted

— maybe it

already has been.

"no, actually it's

max, it's max, like

'where the wild

things are" and i'll

walk home saying

it's max, it's max,

my name is max

we were supposed

to meet on the bus

two years ago.

MAX'S APARTMENT - DAY

Max walks through the frame, coffee mug in hand, to the couch, where she picks up her journal. Voice-over begins as her pen touches the page. There are various images of women beginning their day. These are the main characters of the film, beginning with Max, a twenty-something woman, short and pretty. Next we see various shots of Daria, a bartender in her early twenties. She is a short dark haired spunky woman, wearing her black shirt and Levi's, with a cigarette and sunglasses. She is just getting in. Cut to a woman alone in bed. She has long red hair, she is tall and thin and looks a bit like a hippy. She wears a March on Washington promotional T-shirt. This is Ely, a woman in her late twenties who works as a veterinarian's assistant at a local animal hospital. Last we see Evy and Kia in bed together naked. They shift and reposition. Evy is an attractive Puerto Rican woman in her late twenties. They are a couple newly in love. The voice- over continues as we cut between these images.

Voice-over

I have this great fear that the moment we were supposed to meet will be thwarted—maybe it already has been. I think I saw her on the subway yesterday. I saw her and I thought, we were supposed to meet yesterday, on the bus. She was supposed to sit down next to me, spill her soda on me, and we were supposed to laugh, make a game of cleaning it up where we touch each other more than necessary, coincidentally get off at the same stop, get to talking, and then there's the moment where she says "Well . . . " like she feels dumb because we really don't even know each other and we've been talking like old friends and that's when I realize how excellent she is in every way. And we kiss right there in the street and it's a moment we talk about for years later—how we never believed in love at first sight until we met each other.

Instead some fat man got in the way. She was rushing for the bus and he waddled in front of her, she tried to get around him, spilled the drink she was supposed to spill in my eager lap on his indifferent shoulder, and she missed the bus, which had me on it, with an empty seat next to me, oblivious, thinking about something like the texture of raisins and scraping at the chunk of gum stuck to the seat in front of me.

In fact, I'm sure this is what happened. The whole fiasco probably threw us both way out of whack. Now our paths won't cross until years later when she's forgotten she's a dyke, and she'll move in next door to me, and I'll have a painful crush on her, and she'll be sitting on her porch with her boyfriend and she'll wave to me. I'll be getting my mail, and get a little lilt in my stomach when she waves, and I'll trip over my cat, and stumble in a kind of a three stooges way, and she'll look away like she's embarrassed for me, and I'll go inside and feel really dumb.

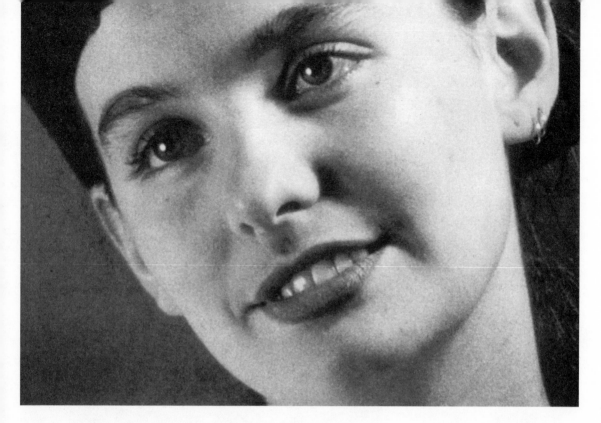

Then her boyfriend will think I seem like I would be fun and one morning when we bump into each other in front of my house he'll invite me to a "shindig" they're having—I'll go and not know anyone and sit in a corner and play with pistachio shells and give each woman there a make-over in my head. ("What if she wore baggy jeans?" "She'd be really hot if she cut off that perm and stopped giggling so much.") Then dreamgirl will introduce me to someone—she'll say "This is Matt— she's my neighbor." and I'll say "No, actually it's Max, it's Max, like 'Where the Wild Things Are'" and I'll walk home saying it's Max, it's Max, my name is Max we were supposed to meet on the bus two years ago. At this very moment we're supposed to be sitting on our couch together reading and playing footsie absentmindedly. My name is Max. I want to borrow your T-shirts and wake you up when I have bad dreams, burst into a smile when we're fighting because you're too adorable, pinch your butt when you're walking up the stairs in front of me. Make up a name that only you call me. Make it something you'd be embarrassed to call me accidentally in public. Fall in love with me. We were supposed to meet so long ago. We're way behind. It's Max. My name is Max.

An alarm clock goes off.

MAX'S APARTMENT - KIA'S BEDROOM

Kia and Evy are in bed. Kia shuts off the alarm clock, puts on her glasses and looks at the time. She is alarmed, but not surprised.

KIA

Shit. . . Evy? Evy baby wake up. I was supposed to be in front of class ten minutes ago.

Kia gets out of bed, Evy right behind her.

EVY

Oh—we're not so late.

Evy moves close and kisses Kia.

KIA

Stop it, you . . . this is why we're in trouble anyway. No more sex after midnight.

                    EVY

    Ohhh . . . I'm not wearing those—do you have any socks?

They both quickly dress.

                    KIA

    Yeah they're in the top drawer over there. Baby have you seen
my lesson planner?

                    EVY

    No, I haven't. Why don't you ask Max?

INT. COMMON AREA - KIA AND MAX'S APARTMENT

Kia and Evy emerge from the bedroom at a quickened pace. Kia wears
a shirt, slacks and the ever-present blazer. Evy wears a hospital uni-
form, I.D. on her collar. Kia walks over to Max's bedroom, still adjust-
ing her thrown-on clothes.

                    KIA

    Max? Max are you up?

Max pokes her head out of her bedroom.

                    MAX

    Yeah—what's goin' on?

                    KIA

    Have you seen my lesson planner? You know, the yellow
thingee?

Max leads as she and Kia walk into the kitchen to retrieve her lesson
planner.

                    MAX

    Ummm . . . I think it's on top of the fridge. I'll get it.

                    KIA

    Why didn't you wake us up?

stop it, you . . . this is why were in trouble anyway. no more sex after midnight.

43

evy hands up the phone. she is upset upset upset upset upset upset upset upset upset upset and leans against the wall wall wall wall wall wall wall wall wall wall

MAX

I'm not going to barge into the love nest.

Max grabs a yellow folder from the top of the refrigerator and hands it to Kia, who tosses it on the table.

MAX

Here it is.

KIA

Where? Oh. Thanks.

MAX

So you remember we're supposed to be meeting tonight, right?

KIA

What?

MAX

We're supposed to be meeting and your gonna read my paper, remember? It's getting published. . .

Evy moves through the kitchen on her way to the bathroom.

EVY

Good morning Max.

MAX

Hey Evy.

EVY

Oh, you found it.

KIA

Yeah, I did. Don't forget to call your Mom.

EVY

I won't.

KIA

Now. What?

Kia prepares a bagel for herself, absentmindedly wrapping it and leaving it on top of the yellow lesson planner.

MAX

5:00, Fanta Cafe, you're reading my paper. You already said yes—you have to come.

KIA

OK, 5:00.

Evy is on the phone, pacing and speaking to her mother. Kia walks past her into the bedroom.

EVY

Mom, I have to go to work, one more shift, then I'll be home at night—I'll be home this evening. For sure, there's no double shifts tonight. There's just— it's just been really busy, and there's a lot of people quitting and . . . OK, Mom—Si, si, como no—Te vea en el noche— bye.

Evy hangs up the phone. She is upset and leans against the wall.

EVY

My Mom says Junior was over again last night.

KIA

I don't understand why he's always over there . . .

EVY

Me neither.

Evy lost in thought continues leaning against the wall. Kia is impatient but attempts to be tender.

this place is like dyke-o-rama. what is it— free rama refills if you've ever kissed a woman?

KIA

Baby—we gotta go.

Evy snaps out of her trance, grabs her backpack and heads for the door.

EVY

OK—my bag. Bye Max.

Max notices Kia has left not only her yellow lesson planner, but her bagel as well. She grabs it and runs for the door.

MAX

See ya, Evy. Oh Kia? Kia, Kia . . .

KIA

Thanks, I'll see you at 5.

MAX

See ya.

Door closes, Max walks off frame.

CAFE - EVENING

Close up of a waitress who leads the camera through the cafe, refilling coffee cups. There are an unusual number of women in the cafe. We come upon Max and Kia sitting at a table.

MAX

This place is like dyke-o-rama. What is it—free refills if you've ever kissed a woman?

The waitress approaches the table and Max takes notice of her.

WAITRESS

Who had the root beer?

MAX

Me. Thanks.

Max stares.

WAITRESS

Coffee?

Max continues to stare.

KIA

Yes, thank you—just a little.

MAX

She is really cute.

KIA

Yea, I don't know, ever since they opened it's been like this,
it's kind of cool but it's a lot of the same old crusty broads.

Max finally turns her attention from the long departed waitress to Kia.

it's kind of cool
but its a lot of
the same old
crusty broads.
broads.

i was a dyke when you were in diapers, kiddo.

you haven't dipped into the honey pot in a while.

MAX

Wait, you mean you know some of these chicks?

KIA

Yeah, most.

MAX

So, what are you like too cool to say hi?

KIA

Who would you like, most attractive to least?

MAX

Now how do you think that's gonna work— we have totally different tastes in women.

KIA

Are you saying I don't have discriminating taste in women? I was a dyke when you were in diapers, kiddo. I, my dear, know what a mature, attractive woman is, but I'm not so sure I'm willing to share that with you now.

MAX

Hey—don't call me kiddo, grandma.

KIA

And what does that say about my lover, I thought you said you wanted to jump her bones when you met her—so what makes you think we have such different taste in women?

MAX

Weird coincidence. Even weirder that she came on to you first.

Kia sits back in her chair, taking on an authoritative pose.

KIA

Anyway—I don't know if I want to leave the two of you alone together—I mean you haven't dipped into the honey pot in a while.

i can't believe that you are
calling me seventies when you're
using such victorian language
~~for sex belief that you are's~~
~~calling me seventies when you're~~
~~using such victorian language~~
for sex. slept with? max, it's
sex. sex. sex as in safe sex. sex
as in fucking, as in making love...

Max reels back in disbelief at the word "honey pot."

MAX

The honey pot? God you are so seventies sometimes, and I would appreciate it if you didn't cut on my nun life-style.

KIA

Try again, Max, at least those nuns are getting some.

Max sits up in her chair.

MAX

Why are you taunting me? I don't need to be reminded every day that I haven't slept with a woman in 10 months.

KIA

I can't believe that you are calling me seventies when you're using such Victorian language for sex. Slept with? Max, it's Sex. Sex as in safe sex, sex as in fucking, as in making love . . .

Kia is on a roll.

i don't need
to be
reminded
every day
that i haven't
slept with a
woman in 10
months.

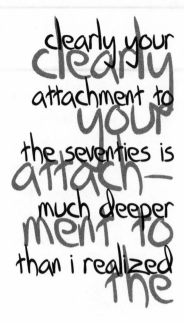

MAX

You can stop now. Maybe I would be more familiar with the terminology if I remembered what it was like, so why don't you facilitate the process by helping me meet some hot babes. Now, the question was, tell me who do you think is the cutest, and can you introduce us?

KIA

Well, first tell me who you wish you could be introduced to.

MAX

No, you tell.

KIA

Go, it's your libido

MAX

Just go—tell me, who?

KIA

Well, OK, let's see. I pick contestant number 1, that woman right over there with the flowing locks. She's adorable.

Kia points to a woman sitting behind Max, Ely. She sits alone reading a book (Backlash). Max steals a glance at her and turns back to Kia looking very disappointed

MAX

Yeah? Clearly your attachment to the seventies is much deeper than I realized.

KIA

Max, she's really nice, she used to go out with a friend of mine.

Max crosses her arms and sits back in her chair.

MAX

I have one word for you: u-g-l-y. She ain't got no alibi—she's ugly, her momma said she's ugly . . .

Max is bobbing her head and singing. Kia is appalled.

                    KIA

        Max, that is so uncalled for—cut it out.

Max is silenced by Kia's reprimand. They sit in silence. Max sips her root beer.

INT. CAFE - LATER THE SAME EVENING

Max and Kia are getting ready to leave. The camera follows them and sees that the seat where Ely was sitting is empty. Max continues to behave remorsefully.

                    MAX

        Thanks so much for looking at my paper— that was cool of you.

                    KIA

No problem.

                    MAX

Hey—are you still talking to me?

KIA

Eventually—I can never stay mad at you long.

Kia leads as she and Max walk to the cash register. On her way out of the cafe is Ely, who has just finished paying.

KIA

Ely, hi, I thought that was you. How are you?

ELY

Good, Kia, how are you doing?

KIA

Fine.

ELY

You're still teaching, right?

KIA

Yeah, I'm still teaching—how's Kate?

ELY

Kate's fine—she's staying in Seattle right now. She keeps threatening to come and visit. But . . . I know she'd like to see you when she comes in.

Max stands in the background, becoming increasingly irritated that Kia has not introduced her to Ely.

KIA

Great. Well, how have you been doing?

ELY

Pretty good. You know I have a job at a vet, pretty much full time, so it's keeping me pretty busy, and actually I'm kinda on my way there right now—so . . .

Max butts in, introducing herself.

MAX

Hi I'm Max, Kia's roommate

Ely shyly shakes Max's hand.

ELY

Hi Max, it's nice to meet you, I'm Ely.

MAX

Hi.

Ely shifts a bit, seeming slightly tense, and inches toward the door.

                    ELY

        Umm . . . well . . . it was nice to see you guys.

Ely has the door open.

                    KIA

        Yeah, it was good seeing you. Give me a call so we can get
together.

                    ELY

        I will.

Ely leaves.

                    KIA

        OK, bye.

Kia and Max turn toward the register. Max turns back to look at Ely walk
away.

                    MAX

        I didn't know you knew her.

                    KIA

Yeah she used to go out with a friend of mine.

                    MAX

              (Smugly)

Well she's never going out with this friend of yours.

                    KIA

Max—get over yourself.

Kia slaps her money on the counter.

CUT TO: BLACK

Voice-over

Sound of a roulette wheel spinning, quickly as we see images of Max with various women, looking quite content. The sound of the wheel slows down. It slows, then stops. It is Max and Ely staring straight ahead.

                    MAX

    Kia, who's this chick we're going out with again? Kia? Ohhhh
. . .

ELY'S APARTMENT - DAY

A closed door, as perky footsteps bounce down stairs. A bell rings. The door is opened to reveal Max standing alone, looking self-conscious, leaning against the door jam.

                    ELY

    Hi Max.

MAX

Hi, sorry I'm late.

Ely looks beyond Max, searching for Kia and looking kind of fidgety. She stands in the doorway with her arms folded.

ELY

Is Kia parking the car?

MAX

No, actually she had to do study plans at the last minute—I don't know why she didn't tell me.

ELY

Well, um . . . do you still want to go?

Ely shifts her weight.

MAX

Umm, well, I guess maybe we should wait for Kia, she really wanted to see this movie.

Max shuffles from foot to foot.

                    ELY

    Yeah, it was her idea—I have stuff to do anyway.

                    MAX

    Okay. Okay, so I'll see you later.

Max steps off the porch and inches backward toward the steps.

                    ELY

    Yeah—we can do it another time.

At that moment Daria walks into frame. She is exiting the apartment with sunglasses on and a girl on her arm. She walks past Max, who suddenly seems very shy.

                    ELY

    Hey you guys.

                    MIMI

    Hi.

max looks
at the
ground,
barely
making
eye con-
tact max
looks very
uncom-
fortable

                              DARIA

                    Hey girl.

Daria stands close to Max and looks her up and down. Max looks at the
ground, barely making eye contact.

                              MAX

                    Hey.

                              DARIA

                    It's Max, right?

                              MAX

                    Yeah.

                              DARIA

                    Lookin' cute as usual—how are ya?

Max looks very uncomfortable.

                              MAX

                    Good. Thanks.

                              DARIA

                    This is Mimi. Max. You know Ely, right?

                              MAX

                    Hi.

                              MIMI

                    Yes.

                              ELY

                    We've met.

Daria steps back and addresses both Ely and Max, who have been
forced to move closer together.

DARIA

So are you two just gonna hang out on the doorstep all night, or what?

MAX

No, I was just leaving. We were gonna go see a movie, but . . .

Max shifts uncomfortably.

DARIA

That's cool. We're going to the Burrito Palace. I'd invite you along but I can see you have some exciting plans of your own.

Daria heads up the step with Mimi.

DARIA

See you later.

MIMI

Bye—nice to meet you.

ELY

Bye you guys.

MAX

Bye.

Max and Ely stand in the doorway. They have to say good-bye again, and the feeling is even more awkward.

ELY

Max, I'm sorry—I didn't mean to make you stand out here. Do you want to come in and have a drink or something?

MAX

No, I'm fine. Thanks though.

 59

Again Max inches toward the steps.

                              ELY

        Okay, well—bye.

                              MAX

        Bye, sorry about this.

                              ELY

        It's okay—it's not your fault—it's no big deal.

                              MAX

        OK.

                              ELY

        Some other time.

                              MAX

        Bye.

The door is once again shut. Off camera we hear the sound of perky
footsteps bounding down the stairs. The door bell rings several times.
Ely enters frame and opens the door to reveal Max standing there, smiling.

                              ELY

        Hi.

                              MAX

        Hi, you know I was thinking—you wanna just go see it? I think,
umm, Kia's just trying to get rid of me so she can have sex with Evy on
the kitchen table or something.

                              ELY

        That sounds like Kia. Alright, I'll go get my stuff.

                              MAX

        Ooh, you have some dirt.

60 ⋯

INT. ELY'S APARTMENT - MOMENTS LATER

Max waits for Ely in silence, shifting her weight from one foot to the other as Ely finally enters frame. They exit the apartment in silence.

INT. ELY'S APARTMENT - NIGHT

Max and Ely are returning from the movie. They walk into the apartment. Max is raving, gesticulating. Ely listens silently.

                    MAX

        That movie sucked. Why do queers always have to be so pathetic? I mean, I'm queer and I'm finding it relatively easy not to hate myself. I mean the man is a gay filmmaker; I feel like he has a certain responsibility to represent us in a positive way.

They walk through the apartment and into the kitchen. Ely goes into her bedroom as Max continues to talk. Ely turns to join Max in the kitchen.

                    ELY

        I don't know, I really liked the film, there were so many beautiful things about it. We expect queer filmmakers to take the responsibility to represent the entire community and I think that's really a lot to ask anyone.

                    MAX

        I know, but I just don't feel like we can withstand such negative representation from within our own ranks—do you know what I mean?

Max removes her hat and runs her hand through her hair. Both women stand in the kitchen rather close to each other.

                    ELY

        Well, if he hates himself for being gay— I mean a lot of people do. I think we want him to represent everyone, and he's just representing what he sees in the community. Do you want some tea or something?

Ely steps toward the stove, pointing Max in the direction of the choices in tea.

that movie sucked.   why
do queers always have to
be so pathetic? i mean,
i'm queer and i'm finding
it relatively easy not to
hate myself.   i mean the
man is a gay filmmaker; i
feel like he has a certain
responsibility to repre-
sent us in a positive way.

I don't know. I really
liked the film, there
were so many beautiful
things about it. We
expect queer filmmakers
to take the responsibility
to represent the entire
community and I think
that's really a lot to
ask anyone.

camera pans
across about
twenty
different
kinds of tea.

MAX

Sure, that would be great.

ELY

There's a bunch of different kinds back there if you wanna pick out something.

Camera pans across about twenty different kinds of tea.

MAX

Wow—you have a lot of tea. You have a lot of tea back there—you like tea?

The mood is becoming lighter, as if they are each starting to see the other's charm.

ELY

I like tea. Did you pick out what kind you want?

MAX

Actually, I'm kind of in the mood for something cold.

ELY

OK. Iced tea?

Both women laugh. Ely reaches into the refrigerator.

                    MAX

That would be great. Can we not say the word tea anymore?

                    ELY

Alright.

                    MAX

Don't say tea.

                    ELY

You wanna go into the living room?

                    MAX

Sure.

Ely and Max walk into the living room. Ely shuts off the lights in the apartment as they head for the couch.

                    MAX

So—you're like a vet?

max is

definitely

flirting

okay so my little brother had

then I forgot about
this really smelly guinea pig

box out in the sun, and

and i wanted to clean up the
the guinea pig out in a

—it cage, so umm, i put it the

wanted to clean up the
guinea pig out in a box out in

smelly guinea pig and !

the sun, and then I forgot
brother had this really

all about it and it just baked.

ELY

I wish—more like a nurse's aide.

Max is definitely flirting.

MAX

Does that mean that you take little bandages and out them on little kitty paws and stuff all day?

ELY

Uh huh. You know, wheel around the jello cart, fluff up their pillows at night.

Ely is definitely flirting.

MAX

Do you give them bed pans?

ELY

My favorite part.

Max sits on the couch. A moment later Ely joins her after shutting off the light in the living room.

MAX

So then I guess that means you'd hate me if I told you that I once killed a guinea pig.

They sit close. Soft music begins in the background.

ELY

Oh. No—I wouldn't hate you. Everyone likes to tell me these grisly animal stories

MAX

But I can tell you, right?

ELY

Yes.

MAX

Okay, so my little brother had this really smelly guinea pig and I wanted to clean up the cage, so umm, I put it—the guinea pig out in a box out in the sun, and then I forgot about it, and it just baked.

Ely smiles and is amused.

ELY

Oh, yuck. That's pretty bad. I once ran over a snake with a lawn mower.

MAX

Gross.

ELY

It was gross. It split it in two—but it lived.

MAX

The snake lived?

ELY

Yeah. It lived. We taped it back together and it sort of grew and lived.

Max moves towards Ely tentatively, withdraws. Ely moves in towards her and they kiss. Giggle.

MAX

Liar.

ELY

No it did, it lived. What is this?

Ely reaches for a charm Max is wearing around her neck.

oh, yuck. that's pretty bad. i once ran over a snake with a lawn mower.

MAX

Oh, it's a good luck charm—my ex-girlfriend gave it to me.

ELY

It's really cute—do you wear it all the time?

MAX

Yeah—actually, I do—I don't know why— it's kind of skanky—don't look at it. Umm—what's this?

Max pulls the charm out of Ely's hand and tucks it back in her shirt. She touches the pendant Ely wears around her neck.

ELY

It's like a thing I got at Michigan, you know, the black triangle.

MAX

It's cool.

Max is still holding the pendant in her hand as the phone rings in the next room.

ANSWERING MACHINE (DARIA)

Hey—I'm still free for Friday night—so whoever leaves the sexiest message gets to win a date with me. You can also leave messages for Ely.

68

                    MAX

Is that Daria on the answering machine?

                    ELY

Yeah, I never leave those messages.

                    MAX

She's so funny.

               ANSWERING MACHINE

          (KATE)

     Hi Sweetie—it's me—are you there? Call me when you get
in—I have great news. I'm missing you today. Call me.

Max slowly lets go of the pendant. Ely seems nervous and rubs her
glass causing it to squeak. Max senses Ely's nervousness and pulls
away a bit.

                    MAX

Is that your mom?

                    ELY

Umm, it's my partner in Seattle.

At this news Max pulls away from Ely completely, trying to act casual.
Ely continues to rub her glass, looking down as she explains.

                    MAX

Oh, umm—is she on vacation?

                    ELY

No—she lives there.

                    MAX

That's really sad, how long has she been there?

                    ELY

Umm, two and a half years.

four women lay on their backs in a star formation. they are kia, daria, evy and daria's date. they are here to discuss the progress of ely and max.

MAX

Why don't you move out there or something?

ELY

Well, it's kind of complicated, I mean, she left after school to work out there— she had a commitment to work and I needed to stay and finish school and I'm still trying to finish school and she has a really good job so we just . . . it's kind of hard.

The squeak of Ely rubbing her glass is the last thing heard.

NON-SPACE - NON-TIME

Four women lie on their backs in a star formation. They are Kia, Daria, Evy and Daria's date. They are here to discuss the progress of Ely and Max.

DARIA

That date was a bad scene, man.

KIA

I don't think Max likes you very much, Daria.

DARIA

Hey—she'll come around.

EVY

What are we gonna do about this Kate woman?

DARIA

Yeah, that relationship has been over for a while.

KIA

Would you guys please remember that Kate is a friend of mine?

DARIA

She's a friend of mine too, Kia, but I know a dead relationship when I see one.

KIA

Yeah, I guess you're right. I can't believe they're still going out together. It's a perfect example of how lesbians never break up.

DARIA

OK? The old lesbian bed death. They're not even a couple.

KIA

I got a feeling about this Ely and Max thing, though—I think it's gonna work out great.

EVY

I still feel sorry for Ely. I mean Kate calling? Such shitty timing. I don't think we've ever met—who's this?

From their positions the women are introduced to Daria's date du jour.

DARIA

This is Melanie.

it's a perfect
example of how
lesbians never
break up.

it's a perfect
example of how
lesbians never
break up.

i got a feeling
about this ely and
max thing, though
— i think it's gonna
work out great.

i got a feeling
about this ely and
max thing, though
— i think it's gonna
work out great.

i don't know how
much max is elys
type.

i don't know how
much max is elys
type.

get
over
it
daria.
it's
called
"
go
fish
"
not
"
all
you
can
eat."

KIA & EVY

Hi.

MEL

Hi. You can call me Mel.

KIA

Okay Mel.

DARIA

So you know, I don't know how much Max is Ely's type. I think Max might be a little fast for her. Maybe we should call this thing "Daria Goes Fishing."

The women protest Daria's concept and Evy takes the liberty of slapping Daria's head.

EVY

Get over it Daria. It's called "Go Fish" not "All You Can Eat."

All the women laugh.

DARIA

True enough.

EVY

Besides, Ely wasn't exactly trying to get out of that kiss.

KIA

They're a tough pair. Is there some natural disaster that happens during this thing that could force the two of them together? Like getting stuck on a train that stops because of an accident in the rain?

EVY

I don't think so. It looks like its gonna happen the long way.

                           DARIA

    That's cool. As long as I get to have some nookie.

All the women hiss.

                           KIA

    Hey! have some respect for Mel.

                           MEL

    Yeah, please.

Daria reaches for Mel and rubs her cheek.

                           DARIA

    I wasn't talking about Max. Lighten up girls.

KIA AND MAX'S APARTMENT - EVENING

Max paces the floor wielding a squirt gun. Kia sits on the floor, she is
grading papers.

                           MAX

    So you're admitting it—you totally set me up.

                           KIA

    No, I didn't set you up, I really did have to plan for my lectures
for today—It was only after you left that I decided to show a film.

                           MAX

    I knew you'd make up some sort of cheap excuse, and now
you're going to pay.

Max stops pacing, points the squirt gun at Kia and fires.

                           KIA

    Hey—Hey! I want you to reflect on what you've just done—
want you to think about your symbolic violence toward me.

Max sits close to Kia and continues to shoot her.

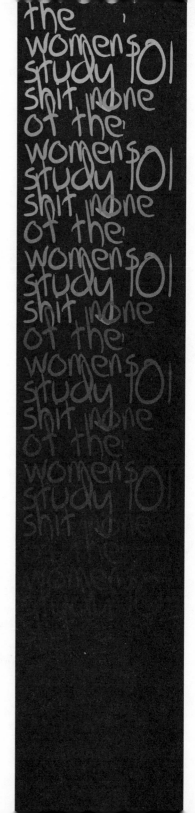

                                    73

MAX

None of that Women's Studies 101 shit.

KIA

This is no laughing matter, missy. This is woman on woman violence and this is very sad.

MAX

No, you know what's sad - is the way you're trying to steer the conversation away from what you did to me.

KIA

OK, OK, Maybe I thought after you got past your shallow fashion requirements you might find Ely interesting.

Max reels in disbelief.

MAX

Kia, interesting!? OK? let me go over the things about her that were really working for me. Dresses like momma in the 70s, has a hundred different kinds of teas, all decaf, she actually liked that stupid movie, she doesn't seem to be interested in her own oppression—and last, and most important—she's married.

KIA

Really to who? To Kate?

MAX

You mean you knew she had a girlfriend?

KIA

No, not really. I mean I thought they broke up—they don't even live in the same city.

MAX

Try two years of not living in the same city. And in all that time they've only visited each other three times.

KIA

Crazy. I remember when Kate was in my class.

MAX

She was? When?

KIA

A couple of years before you.

MAX

What does she look like? Probably a total hippie, right?

dresses like
dresses like
momma in the
momma in the
70s, has a hun—
70s, has a hun—
dred different
dred different
kinds of teas, a
kinds of teas, all
decaf, she actual—
decaf, she actual—
ly liked that stu—
ly liked that stu—
pid movie, she
pid movie, she
doesn't seem to be
doesn't seem to be
interested in her
interested in her
own oppression~
own oppression~
and last, and most
and last, and most
important—she's
important—she's
married.
married.

KIA

No—I'm not even going to start in on this one.

MAX

Just tell me—regular, crunchy, or extra crunchy?

KIA

Max, settle down. I won't say if she's a hippie or not, but keep in mind that she did move to Seattle.

BOTH

Extra Crunchy.

MAX

It doesn't matter anyway. I remain as I have been for quite some time—a carefree, single, lesbo . . .

KIA & MAX

...looking for love.

Max slaps her knees in resolve as she stands up.

KIA

I still think you guys would be good together.

Max sits down again, exasperated.

MAX

Kia, that would be the little relationship that could.

KIA

Max, what have you got to lose?

MAX

Kia, this is so worthless, I wish you'd just admit that.

KIA

Why are they apart if they're so in love?

MAX

You know, in the whole time I was talking to her she never once mentioned love. It was like they were business partners or something. And you know what's even weirder? There's no tangible reason why they should live apart.

KIA

I thought Ely was in school.

MAX

Nope. She told me she quit.

KIA

Crazy. So she's just kinda hanging around keeping Daria company?

MAX

I guess.

KIA

Maybe Ely and Daria - you know...

MAX

Eww, I definitely don't think so. Daria's a ho.

probably
besides,
more out
you
of fear
know she
and inertia
and Kate are
than on
monogamous.
principle.

KIA

Hey—leave Daria alone. What would you rather our collective lesbian image be— Hot passionate say yes to sex dykes or touchy feely soft focus sisters of the woodlands? I mean I think it's important that we acknowledge women who are comfortable with their sexual selves, especially lesbians.

MAX

OK, OK, so Daria's a positive 90s role model and Ely's a little behind the times—still, I don't think they're doing it. Ely seems . . . I

don't know . . . like she's too honest for that. Besides, you know she and Kate are monogamous.

KIA

Ely & Kate? Probably more out of fear and inertia than on principle. Ely's always been a little timid.

MAX

You mean of sex?

KIA

No, it seems less general than that, like she's got this fear of intimacy and she's got herself in this really comfy position where she just doesn't have to confront it.

MAX

I guess that makes sense. I hate this, why is it always like this? I just want to find a girlfriend and have there be no catches, no glitches, no booby traps. . .

Both women laugh. Max sighs deeply.

MAX

Oh, I know, as much as we joke about it I really just want to find a girlfriend.

KIA

I'm sorry, I didn't realize how complicated it would be.

MAX

But you did set me up.

Max once again draws her weapon and prepares to fire.

KIA

Yeah.

Max shoots.

but you did set me up

first it was paula — things that turn her off are squishy bodies and hairy backs. then nikki — she wants a man who isn't a preppy, doesn't have too many muscles and won't bug her. finally julia, in her spare time — she likes to paint her nails and put on day-glo lipstick.

KIA

I deserve it.

Max comes over and crouches next to Kia.

MAX

No you don't deserve it, and you know we really did get along in spite of her severe case of hippitus.

MAX

You know the worst thing about it, the thing that totally makes it suck?

KIA

What?

MAX

I kissed her.

KIA

She kissed you back?

MAX

Yeah.

KIA

Tongue?

Max nods.

KIA

Then I'd say my plan is still working.

Kia grabs Max's squirt gun and pretends she is going to shoot her. Both women laugh.

ELY & DARIA'S APARTMENT - NIGHT

Ely is lying on the couch watching television. She is alone.

Voice-over (television)

[the dialogue happens over the voice-over]

My mother used to express it as "a bubble left of plum,"

another expression for a little off-kilter

OK

Now, what do you mean by off-kilter?

You know, wild, crazy—uh—the example I was thinking was I had met
this one girl and we had gone to a party and it was really a drag and um
the next thing you know we're running naked through the apartment
complex and you know jumpin' in jacuzzis and whatnot and that's kinda
. . . that's it.

That's off-kilter to you, huh?

Yeah it is.

Ely seems almost irritated with what she is watching.

Okay, and you said there was something that a woman MUST tell you up front or that you expect them to tell you up front

Well, actually, it's what I'd like to tell them, and . . .

Oh, you wanna tell them up front . . .

Yeah, it's that I'm here to have a good time, and . . . you know we may have something going but I'm not looking for a life mate or a girlfriend or any kind of serious commitment. I'm just out to go rage for a while.

Okay. We're gonna show everybody that three women that Lance had to choose from for his first date. First it was Paula— things that turn her off are squishy bodies and hairy backs. Then Nikki—she wants a man who isn't preppy, doesn't have too many muscles and wont bug her. Finally, Julia, in her spare time—she likes to paint her nails and put on day-glo lipstick.

Through the sound of the television we hear keys in the door. Ely looks unaffected. She wishes to be left alone. Daria enters, full of energy.

DARIA

Hey girl.

ELY

(slightly irritated)

Hey, Daria

DARIA

Did I get any mail?

ELY

No, nothing.

DARIA

Any phone calls?

ELY

That woman . . . Tracy called.

Daria enters the frame and sits down on the floor next to Ely. Ely looks like she wants to be left alone, but Daria doesn't get it.

DARIA

Oooh.

Daria grabs the Ely's drink and takes a sip. She keeps it.

ELY

Hey, aren't you supposed to be at work?

DARIA

Yeah, but it was dead . . .

Ely looks at Daria drinking her soda.

DARIA

I'll get more.

Ely and Daria both turn their attention toward the television. Ely shifts restlessly, as the program begins speaking of the outcome of a date.

DARIA

I hate this part—you never get to see how the date turns out.

ELY

What difference does it make? You know, it always turns out shitty any way.

Ely gets up off the couch. Daria grabs her hand, concerned, but not really knowing what to do.

DARIA

Is something wrong?

ELY

No, it's OK.

DARIA

You going to bed?

you know miss camille a.k.a. "max" west has got this ideal girlfriend in her head. i think it's some-thing like hip-hop barbie.

                    ELY

        Yeah. See ya.

Ely walks away as Daria continues to hold her hand.

                    DARIA

        Yeah? Okay, good night.

Ely exits.

FADE TO BLACK

NON-SPACE

Four women lay on their backs, facing the camera. They discuss the progress of Ely and Max's relationship.

                    KIA

            This is not looking good. They're both depressed and spend-ing all that time alone. I'm bummed out.

                    EVY

            I just hope this isn't gonna be one of those unrequited love stories.

                    DARIA

            No, listen you guys, everything's gonna work out fine. Ely's just this way, she just has to get really down before she'll do something radical to change her life. I've seen it before. You know we could just forget the whole thing and fix me and Max up.

The woman lying next to Daria (her date for the day) slaps her on the head. Daria chuckles, slightly embarrassed.

                    DARIA

        Oh! You guys, this is Samantha.

Daria rubs Samantha's face in an apologetic manner.

                    KIA & EVY

        Hi.

SAM

Hi. Call me Sam.

KIA

Okay, Hi Sam.

KIA

You know Miss Camille a.k.a. "Max" West has got this ideal girlfriend in her head. I think it's something like hip- hop Barbie. I'm hoping she's gonna do some growing up and start getting into Ely.

Daria laughs, amused by this information.

DARIA

Her real name is Camille? That slays me.

                                  EVY

         Let's get back on track. What in the world is going to make
    them speak to each other again?

                                  KIA

         I have no idea. Why are lesbians so weird?

                                  DARIA

         Tell me about it.

                                  EVY

         I think Ely's a little weird.

                                  DARIA

         She's not weird, she just a little shy.

                                  KIA

         Yeah—how long do you suppose it's been since she's had
    sex?

                                  DARIA

         It's been a long ass time.

    All the women laugh.

                                  EVY

         Is Kate cute?

                                  KIA

         Well, yeah. I mean she's not my type or anything, but she's
    attractive enough.

                                  DARIA

         Woofer.

                                  KIA

         Eye of the beholder, darling.

EVY

Damn, Daria, I wonder what you say about me behind my back?

Daria reaches back and touches Evy's face, lovingly.

DARIA

Only good things.

Kia shoots a look at Daria.

KIA

Let's get on with it. Get away from her.

DARIA & ELY'S APARTMENT - DAY

Open on a white sheet draped over a chair in a sunlit room. Daria spins the chair absentmindedly. She tries to coax Ely into sitting down.

DARIA

Ely, it's gonna be great, you gotta take the risk, I know you're

ready for it. Come on, sit down.

Ely comes into frame and sits. She looks worried.

ELY

It's not like I'm scared. I'm really ready to do this. I just . . .
I'm afraid it's gonna look bad.

Ely pokes nervously at her long hair.

HAIRCUTTER

Come on it's gonna be great. Change is a good thing.

Daria pats Ely, who still does not look convinced.

DARIA

Yeah, you don't have to worry, she's gonna get her license in
about a month. She cuts her own hair even. She knows what she's
doing.

We pan down to see Daria rubbing the head of a woman sitting on the
floor, light hair, small glasses, and only a tuft of hair on the top of her
head. This is Daria's latest chick.

ELY

Alright, you guys can stop. I'm really ready.

DARIA

I'm so proud of you. You haven't had your hair short since
sixth grade when Bobby Saleski put gum in it.

Again Ely fusses with her hair.

ELY

Remember how that looked?

HAIRCUTTER

I think a haircut is definitely something you have to be prepared for in order for it to turn out good.

Daria hugs her girlfriend with new found respect.

DARIA

See, isn't she great—she even knows the psychology of it.

Ely is over it, she is ready.

ELY

I am physically and emotionally ready— let's go.

Daria's girl gets up and grabs the scissors. Ely is getting a haircut. A wacky little tune begins as we see, in a series of shots. Ely's transformation.

A BOOKSTORE - DAY

Camera pans across shelves of books. Max is browsing in one of the aisles, looking at a feminist comic strip. She becomes bored and places the comic back on the shelf, moving to the next aisle. She scopes the other customers, noticing one looks rather familiar. She stares at the short haired woman, (with only a tuft of hair on the top of her head) who also browses in the store. It is Ely with her new haircut. Max goes over to the magazine rack, still staring, pretending to browse. Max picks up a magazine and approaches Ely.

MAX

Hey.

ELY

Hi Max.

MAX

I thought that was you. I was looking at you for the longest time without knowing it was you.

Max rubs Ely's head. Ely seems slightly self conscious, but very endearing.

MAX

Wow. Bold. Sorry.

well, it's a gender bender. your girlfriend's in for a big surprise— you ran away femme and came back a big old butch.

<ELY>

ELY

That's all right. Everybody likes to touch it. I was thinking about getting it cut and then Daria's dating this hairdresser and they kind of talked me into it.

Ely places the book she was looking at back on the shelf.

MAX

I like it. It gives you a really different look.

ELY

You think it looks butch, right?

Max chuckles.

MAX

Well, it is a gender-bender. Your girlfriend's in for a big sur- prise—you ran away a femme and came back a big old butch.

Max pokes Ely with her magazine as she cracks up, but Ely is not amused.

MAX

Hey—that was a joke—you're supposed to laugh.

Ely shifts uncomfortably, half smiling. Max sighs, feeling like she is say- ing one wrong thing after the other.

MAX

I know, the butch/femme thing is really oppressive. Umm, so . . . you weren't trying to look more butch, were ya?

ELY

No, I just wanted to get it cut and then I heard someone said I looked like a hippie and so that pushed it over the edge.

At the word hippie Max steps back in shock and amazement. She bold- ly lies.

MAX

I didn't think you looked like a hippie.

Ely and Max begin walking toward the cashier.

ELY

It's kind of embarrassing—don't tell anyone that's why I cut it. I don't know, I mean, I didn't think you looked like a lesbian when I first saw you. I don't know, what did I need a labrys around your neck or something to tip me off?

MAX

I know, it's funny, it's like I've wanna get my hair cut right now because it's getting a little bit long, but what if people think I'm just cutting it so that I'm like . . . look more like a "real" dyke?

Ely leans by the cash register as they continue to talk. She seems to be feeling a bit more at ease now.

ELY

Yeah, but if you don't cut it, because you want to, aren't you falling into the same trap?

MAX

Totally. But I haven't had a date in ten months anyway. Well, no, there was this one chick I went to a movie with, but she turned out to have a girlfriend, so maybe I do need a haircut.

ELY

Max, I'm sorry about that. I mean, there just didn't seem a good time to tell you.

MAX

It's no big deal—it happens to me all the time.

At this point both women are clearly flirting with each other.

ELY

You should cut your hair—it looks good that way. Besides, look at how you dress.

kia lies

down on

the bed,

reading a

feminist

publication.

MAX

Hey—I'm not dressed this way to look dykey—I'm fashion-able—there is a difference.

ELY

Oh, and I'm not?

MAX

Well, you're kinda leaning toward the hippie side.

ELY

(jokingly)

Better a hippie than a butch wanna be.

MAX

(feinting offense)

Oooh. I'm just kidding—I don't think you look like a hippie. I think you look good—I mean I think you look fine . . .

Max suddenly seems very self conscious. She begins to inch toward the door, magazine still in hand.

MAX

. . . I mean, like not like a hippie. Anyway, it was good to see you and I'll see you later

Max opens the door of the bookstore.

ELY

Okay. See you.

Ely turns towards the cashier, smiling. In the background Max reenters the bookstore, holding the magazine she accidentally walked out with. Ely and Max exchange a moment.

MAX

I forgot to pay.

KIA'S BEDROOM - NIGHT

Kia lies down on the bed, reading a feminist publication. Evy enters the room, robe on, towel wrapped around her head.

                    KIA

    Hey baby.

Kia turns her attention to Evy, who walks past her. She puts moisturizer on her face as she talks.

                    EVY

        Hey, Did you set the alarm? Because if I'm late one more time, I'm gonna be fired.

Kia sits up a bit.

                              KIA

        I think Max has the clock. (Yelling into the apartment) Max?
Max? I think she's asleep already.

Evy steps back and looks toward Max's room.

                              EVY

        No, she's not. I'll go get it.

Evy exits the bedroom. Kia returns to her book. Off-camera we hear the
sound of Evy's footsteps as she reenters the room.

                              EVY

        Boy, that is one serious little roommate you got there.

                              KIA

        What's she up to?

                              EVY

        She's writing—she handed me the clock without even looking
at me.

Evy plugs in the clock and kneels at the side of the bed, next to Kia to adjust the time.

                    KIA

        Mmmm. I'll bet she's thinking about Ely. I think she's afraid
to admit that she likes her.

Evy looks up from her task.

                    EVY

        What, that Max likes Ely, or that Ely likes Max?

                    KIA

        I think that Max likes Ely, and probably Ely likes Max also, but
she's just kind of cautious by nature . . .

Kia shuts her book and puts it on the night stand. She takes off her
glasses and leans back on the pillow. Evy puts the clock down and pulls
the towel off her head.

                    KIA

        . . . maybe not—anyway I hope they get over it soon because
they're kind of at that agonizing stage when two people meet. You
know, is this gonna work, is this person worth it, should I take the
plunge . . .

Evy smiles at her far too analytical girlfriend. She hops on the bed,
simultaneously straddling Kia.

                    EVY

        And what about you? What made you take the plunge when
you first saw me?

                    KIA

        I was drunk.

They kiss.

                    EVY

        Oh you were not.

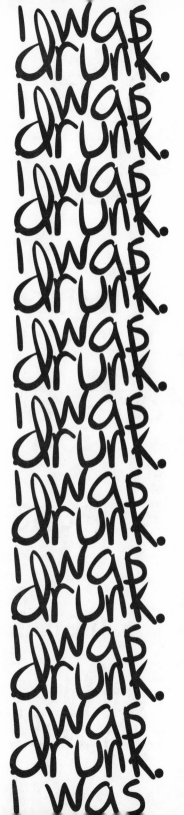

my defi-
nition of
lesbian
does not
involve
men in
any way.

KIA

I was too. Two glasses of wine, that's drunk for me.

They kiss again. Evy sits up on Kia and does a little dance.

EVY

Blame it on the wine. You were enticed by my dancing.

Kia laughs and kisses Evy.

KIA

Was not. You were just playing it up for me because you knew I was watching.

They kiss again.

EVY

Was not.

KIA

You were very sexy.

More kissing.

ELY

Was not.

Kissing, giggling.

FADE TO BLACK:

INT. BEDROOM - NIGHT

The camera shows two bodies in a bed together. It is not clear who they are or what gender they are, but they seem to be at some point of sex. The camera pulls back to reveal Daria, then pulls back further to reveal the person she is having sex with is a man. He kisses her and they begin having sex again.

CUT TO:

EXT. ALLEY - NIGHT

96

Daria is walking alone, and then is suddenly approached and abducted by two women in leather jackets.

CUT TO:

A COURTROOM - NON TIME

Daria finds herself in front of a jury of her piers. Lights are moving quickly. She is being questioned about her most recent sexual exploit. Most of the women in the jury are hostile, and question her in a very accusatory and suspicious manner.

THE JURORS

What do you think you are doing?

It makes me sick.

DARIA

(defensively)

Does it make you sick or does it just scare you?

THE JURORS

Just don't call yourself something that you're not.

DARIA

If you're talking about me calling myself a lesbian, that's what I am.

THE JURORS

My definition of lesbian does not involve men in any way.

THE JURORS

How are we supposed to establish some kind of identity if lesbians are going around having sex with men?

DARIA

Maybe we need to . . .

THE JURORS

What, go out and get some dick?

🐟 97

DARIA

And we're not talking about life commitment here, we're talking about sex. Just sex.

THE JURORS

(righteously)

There's no such thing as "just sex."

THE JURORS

If you sleep with men, I want to know that before I sleep with
you.

DARIA

So you don't have sex with women who've slept with men?

THE JURORS

We're not talking about the past, we're talking about the present.

DARIA

And what is the exact amount of time that has to pass before
I regain my lesbian status?

THE JURORS

I don't have sex with women who sleep with men.

THE JURORS

Yeah, did you have safe sex?

DARIA

Yeah, when's the last time you did?

THE JURORS

Last time I had sex.

DARIA

Anyone else?

There is a silent pause as none of the jurors respond. We hear the sound of wind.

THE JURORS

You can't just do that.

DARIA

Oh come on—he's a friend of mine. What's the big fucking

deal? Women are my life. I love women.

THE JURORS

But you just can't stay away from that dick.

DARIA

Fuck you!

THE JURORS

I'd like to hear her say why she did it.

DARIA

Well I forgot for a minute that Big Sister was watching.

THE JURORS

I just don't see what's so bad about it.

THE JURORS

Yeah—maybe she considers herself bisexual.

THE JURORS

Well then she should say that.

DARIA

But I don't—I'm a lesbian who had sex with a man.

THE JURORS

No such thing.

Daria is becoming increasingly confident of her defense and is taking the opportunity to give her point of view.

DARIA

I had sex with one man. You know, if a gay man has sex with a woman, he was bored, drunk, lonely, whatever.

If a lesbian has sex with a man, her entire life choice becomes suspect. I think it's bullshit. I think you all are giving men way too much importance here.

100 ᴑᴤᴑ

THE JURORS

I think you're making up a bunch of excuses to hide your desire for men. Why not just live your life the way you want to—and don't call yourself a lesbian?

THE JURORS

Yeah. No one would care who you have sex if you just call yourself what you really are.

DARIA

Why don't you all clue me in on what I really am, and I'd be happy to embrace it.

THE JURORS

I think you have to have sex with a man a certain number of times over a period of time to have your identity as a lesbian be questioned.

THE JURORS

I think it's a question of how you do it.

THE JURORS

I don't think she's really a dyke.

THE JURORS

I don't think she's strong enough to be a dyke.

THE JURORS

No—it's cool for her to do what she wants, but I wouldn't date her.

DARIA

And I don't want to date anyone that closed-minded.

THE JURORS

You mean you tell every woman you sleep with how many men you have had sex with, and how recently?

why
is
everyone
acting
like
it's
the
end
of
the
world
for
her
to
have
sex
with
some
stupid
guy

DARIA

No. But I have probably had sex with more women than any-one else in this room, and I'm not saying that quality is quantity, but it's a lot harder to keep your identity as a single lesbian than as a woman who is in some homey little relationship for 12 years.

THE JURORS

Then the women you do have sex with don't know what they're dealing with.

DARIA

What's the likelihood of a woman I meet tonight coming home with me if I say "I think you should know, I recently had sex with a man?"

THE JURORS

Very slim.

DARIA

Exactly.

THE JURORS

Exactly what? It would be dishonest not to tell her.

Daria is frustrated. There seems to be no way of making these women understand her motivation.

THE JURORS

Who the hell wants to think about all the people the person they're having sex with has had sex with?

THE JURORS

I don't know, some people get off on that.

THE JURORS

No, the point is, I think she's cute enough, but if I thought she was going to have some sudden urge to have sex with a man while I was dating her, I'd say forget it.

DARIA

If you and I were in some committed relationship, I wouldn't be having sex with anyone but you.

THE JURORS

But whose to say this whim won't pop up again?

DARIA

I don't cheat on people.

THE JURORS

Why is everyone acting like it's the end of the world for her to have sex with some stupid guy?

THE JURORS

I hate to picture her having sex with a guy.

THE JURORS

If it means so little to you, why are you acting so guilty?

THE JURORS

Did you enjoy it?

DARIA

(dispassionately)

It wasn't bad.

THE JURORS

Did you come?

DARIA

No.

THE JURORS

But I'll bet he did.

i
wasn't
in
it
for
the
orgasm.

DARIA

I wasn't in it for the orgasm.

THE JURORS

What were you in it for?

DARIA

Sex.

CUT TO:

EXT. ALLEY - NIGHT

Daria continues walking down the dark alley. She looks even more dis-
turbed than before. She runs her hand through her hair and tries to
shake what she has just imagined.

NON-SPACE - NON-TIME

Three women, Daria, Evy and Kia lay on their backs, facing the camera.
It is another meeting to scheme about Ely and Max.

EVY

Hey Daria—why have you been so quiet today?

DARIA

Just thinkin'.

KIA

Where's your lucky dream date for the week?

DARIA

It's been a slow week.

EVY

It's been rough on all of us. But, have we got a girl for you.

At this Evy pulls out a cute little mannequin head and passes it over to Daria.

DARIA

Oh, you guys.

Daria places the mannequin head next to her and snuggles up. Now they are four heads.

EVY

This is Marianna. Marianna, meet Daria.

DARIA

She's so glamorous.

KIA

It's love.

DARIA

You know, I think I've had this girl before.

The head has helped, the mood is lighter and all the women laugh.

KIA

Okay, hey hey kids, what about Ely and Max?

butch

butch

butch

butch

butch

butch

butch

EVY

They seem to be making some progress.

DARIA

But Max should not have said the word "butch" to her. She's very sensitive about that.

KIA

I liked Ely's hair better long.

DARIA

No way. It's awesome in a crew cut.

EVY

Yeah, Max thinks so too. Did you see the way she touched it?

KIA

Yeah but I still think Ely needs to relax a little.

EVY

Definitely.

EXTERIORS - DAY

(no dialogue)

A melancholy song begins as each of the main characters is alone in her daily life. Max shops, headphones on. Ely walks several dogs, and later closes up shop at the animal hospital. Evy is getting off of work and is on her way home to her mother's house. Daria is seen walking into the bar she works at. She cleans up, restocks, smokes, poses and waits for business. Kia walks down the street, briefcase in hand, on her way to class. As she walks down the street someone screams off camera, "What a fuckin' dyke!" Kia responds, "Hey, fuck you!"

        DISSOLVE INTO:

INT. MAX & KIA'S APARTMENT - DAY

Max sits in a chair, crossed legged, deep in thought. She begins writing in her journal. As she writes, the following images are on screen.

        CUT TO:

INT. VACANT INDUSTRIAL SPACE - NON-TIME

Max occupies a space with about five other women. They stand in various formations as the camera examines them. Max and each of the other women appear in a wedding gown. Max is standing alone. The women wearing the dress are approached and kissed by the other women present, as though they are saying good-bye and not congratulations. The voice-over is heard throughout.

Voice-over

What if one day the feeling of having a dirty secret overwhelms me—
what if I crack under the strain of never being out enough (how can I be
out to the woman I'm standing next to at the bus stop, the child who
smiles at me in the store, the man who asks me to spare a quarter?)
What if I black out and I wake up alone midday in a house and I've been
napping and find I'm married to a man—an honest man, who is devot-
ed to me and I'm late to pick up the kids. What if all I do is sigh
because it's not as late as I thought and I race off to pick up the kids
with two umbrellas because it's raining but it wasn't this morning and I
don't want them to catch a cold this early in the season.

I imagine the joy of kissing my husband in the supermarket and the
wistful smile of the old woman who sighs quietly "young love." Mother
insists that we come to her house for Thanksgiving because "it feels so
good to have a man around the house again at holidays." I can sink
into the comfort of being mother, wife, sister-in-law, grandmother—not
always off to the side, un-coupled in a family portrait—not strapped
with the awkward title of aunt.

I could live a life of gender-specific pronouns and answer truthfully
about boyfriends and mean only "good friend" when I say it, and leave
off that desperate qualifier, "really good friend."

Sex would be a friendly ritual, always finite, never frightening, I could
focus on respect while he fucked me—how I know he respects me and
how if really feels kind of good if you eradicate the underlying image of
the empty hole longing to be filled and try not to dwell on the satisfac-
tion he thinks he's getting from filling it.

Double income; I could keep my own name, maybe hyphenate for a lib-
erated feel—we could have anniversary dinners in lovely spots and he'd
dash off to the waiter while I'm in the ladies' room so they can bring
out an anniversary treat before the bill and the waitstaff will feel a warm
glow.

What if I find myself with a more weathered face in a park, laughing,
saying "I was so young", holding hands with a parka and old spice who
squeezes my hand and says, "I feel better, honey, knowing you've tried
everything and still choose me."

It doesn't seem so far-fetched—like being caught in cross-fire and dying
or slipping on oil that someone else unwittingly spilled. I could chase
a rabbit through the woods for sport and find myself falling down a long
dark hole which ends in a life from which I can't escape.

It's the word "phase." It's finally coming out but still being called "gay."
It's being fucked and sucked by a woman until you feel you could cry,

*im not waiting for a
man. i just hate this
eerie feeling that a
man is waiting for me.*

all the while feeling in the back of your mind that no one knows what you really do. We're not waiting for a man. I'm not waiting for a man. I just hate this eerie feeling that a man is waiting for me.

On the last words of the voice-over, several women are lined up, staring into the camera for a moment and then walking off. They stare defiantly. The last woman in line has a more tentative look, and she is wearing the wedding dress.

EVY'S MOTHER'S HOUSE - DAY

As Evy approaches her mother's home, the words "man is waiting for me" repeat. She enters the apartment and sees that her ex-husband Junior is sitting at the table having coffee with her mother. Her mother stands by the sink. She looks angry.

> JUNIOR
>
> George and I were out last night on the town . . .

> EVY
>
> Hi Mommy.

Evy approaches her mother, but turns to Junior first, angry at his presence.

> EVY
>
> What are you doing here? Don't you have a house?

> JUNIOR
>
> Don't you have a life?

Evy attempts to give her mother a kiss. Her mother recoils, pushing Evy away.

> MOTHER
>
> No me besa. Sientate. Quiero habla contigo.

Evy definitely suspects something is up. She sits down very tentatively. She's worried.

> MOTHER
>
> Evelisa, where were you last night?

Evy looks at her mother and stutters out an answer.

                    EVY

        I . . . I was with Marta.

Her mother slaps her.

                    MOTHER

        Mentirosa! Junior told me where you was at last night. He
said he saw you in one of those . . . those gay bars.

Evy shoots a look at Junior, who returns it with a smug, self-righteous
look.

                    MOTHER

        Is it true? Is it true?

Evy sits in silence, looking at the floor. Her mother grabs her chin, waiting for an answer. She takes Evy's silence as a positive response, and
she is beside herself.

                    MOTHER

        Oh my God, is that how I brought up, to become a pata, is this
what I taught you? Ay, no me digas. No wonder Junior left you.

Evy's mother starts pacing and gesticulating wildly. She is shocked and
angry.

                    EVY

        Is that what he told you, is that what you said, you liar?

                    MOTHER

        Shut-up. Deja le quieto.

Evy attempts to get up, but her mother pushes her back down into her
seat.

                    EVY

        I can't believe this.

no wonder
junior left you

you sleep with
women? you
kiss women?
what do you
think you are —
a man?

lll

MOTHER

Listen, so what you are? You sleep with women? You kiss women? What do you think you are—a man?

Evy gets up again. She desperately wants to leave. Her mother grabs her.

EVY

Mommy, you don't understand . . .

Evy's mother is shaking her.

MOTHER

No you don't understand—as long as you live in my house you are going to go by my rules!

Junior attempts to break the two women apart. He did not expect Evy's mother to react so violently.

JUNIOR

Deja la!

MOTHER

Suerta me, chico.

As Evy's mother brushes off Junior, Evy escapes from her grip and runs for the door.

EVY

I'm getting the hell out of here.

Evy grabs her backpack and heads out.

MOTHER

Where are you going?

The mother is shocked that Evy is leaving.

EVY

I'm getting out of here.

Evy's mother follows her to the door, yelling after her.

                    MOTHER

          Si tu te vas ahora, no te ... nunca na mas.

In the doorway, Evy turns and yells at Junior.

                     EVY

          Junior, you're a fucking asshole!

Evy runs down the steps. Her mother yells after her.

                    MOTHER

          Evelisa, it doesn't matter what I see anyway, it's what God
sees, he's watching you—you're gonna have to answer to him— if you
leave now, forget it, don't you come back here.

Evy's mother reels in disbelief. Junior comes forward, closes the door
and locks it.

                    JUNIOR

          Just let her go.

          CUT TO: BLACK

THE STREET - LATE DAY

Evy is distraught. She is on her way to Kia's. She is thinking of her relationship with her mother. She is sad.

Voice-over (in Spanish)

                     GIRL

          I want to be a teacher

                    WOMAN

          What kind of teacher?

                     GIRL

          A music teacher.

you're a
fucking
asshole!

                    WOMAN

And why do you want to be a teacher?

                    GIRL

Because I like my music teacher the best and I want to be like
her.

                    WOMAN

And you will have a house?

                    GIRL

I don't know, maybe.

                    WOMAN

And what will your husband be like? Tall, like Papa?

                    GIRL

No, because . . . because . . . I don't want him to be like Papa
because Papa doesn't yell, but he doesn't talk much either.

                    WOMAN

And where will you live?

                    GIRL

I want to live in a house with my best friend.

                    WOMAN

Do you love me?

                    GIRL

Yes, I love you very much.

During the voice-over we see Evy going over to Kia's house intercut with
Max doing the dishes and listening to music on her Walkman. Evy looks
desperate while Max is bobbing to the music. The voice over ends when
Evy rings the doorbell.

MAX & KIA'S APARTMENT - DAY

114

The door bell rings, but Max does not hear it because of her Walkman.
Evy is becoming increasingly frustrated as she bangs on the door outside. Finally Max hears something and goes to the window to see who
it is. She sees a very distraught Evy pacing the landing of her building.

                    EVY

Shit.

                    MAX

Evy man, why don't you use the doorbell?

                    EVY

Max can you let me in please?

MAX

Yeah, just a sec.

Evy continues pacing as Max comes down the stairs to let her in.

MAX

Hi.

Evy walks in without even saying hello to Max. Max appears clueless. Both women head up the stairs toward Kia and Max's apartment.

MAX

Kia's not home. She should be back around seven.

At this news, Evy gives up. She turns and sits on the steps, too disappointed to go the rest of the way. Max is surprised and turns to sit with Evy.

EVY

Oh shit!

MAX

Evy—what's going on? Is something wrong?

Max really does not know what to do. She reaches out to comfort Evy,

but stops short of making contact with her shoulder before she withdraws her hand once again.

                    EVY

     It's fucked up, Max. Junior told my mom everything. She kicked me out of the house. You know, he fucking set me up, and he's sitting there, waiting for shit to come down. He knows my Mom isn't gonna understand. And now she never wants to see my face again. I can't believe this.

                    MAX

     Holy shit.

Max is trying to figure out the appropriate response. Evy is frustrated and angry.

                    EVY

     Where the fuck is Kia!!?

Max tries being angry too.

                    MAX

     Man, you know, I'd like to get that guy, and get a big pack of dykes and corner him in an alley and make him beg each and every one of us not to kill him, and then fucking kill him anyway.

This is not what Evy needs at the moment, but there is no stopping Max as she has her revenge fantasy.

                              MAX

Evy, man, we should squash him, we should get revenge on him. I can't believe the nerve of him to get you kicked out of your own house...

                              EVY

Max, Max, please be quiet. You never know when to be quiet.

                              MAX

                         (remorsefully)

Oh. I'm sorry Evy. What do you want me to do?

Again, Max reaches out to comfort Evy, but she retracts before making contact.

                              EVY

I don't know.

Max looks off again, forgetting herself.

                              MAX

That guy must just have NO fucking life. No life at all . . .

Evy cuts Max off almost immediately.

                              EVY

Max, Max, shut up Max.

                              MAX

I'm sorry Evy—I just can't get over what a dick he is.

                              EVY

Max, listen, I just got kicked out of the house. My mom thinks I'm going to hell. I don't have a place to live. I don't really give a fuck about Junior.

Finally, Max touches Evy's shoulder, in a reassuring manner.

                    MAX

        But Evy, you know you can live with us. We can be your new
family.

                    EVY

        Fine.

INT. LAUNDRY ROOM - DAY

Ely meticulously picks the whites out of her laundry basket, inspecting
each before she tosses it in the washing machine. Daria leans on the
dryer, watching her. She takes a swig of her root beer, and shakes her
head.

                    DARIA

        Man, Ely, you really need to loosen up girl, chill out, maybe get
laid . . .

                    ELY

                (sarcastically)

        Ooh, is that a proposition?

                    DARIA

                (kiddingly)

        Yeah. No really, babe, when are you gonna get back into the
fray, start mating again?

                    ELY

                (exasperated)

        Daria, you know I have a partner.

                    DARIA

        You do not have a partner. You have a really good excuse and
it's getting kinda weak.

                    ⌖ 119

let's not talk about it, you know i can't do this non-mono-gramous hip thing.

no you can't, because in order for you to be non-monoga- mous you have to be having sex even with one person, for starters, right!

ELY

Let's not talk about it. You know I can't do this non-monoga- mous, hip thing.

Ely continues sorting her laundry, a bit more rapidly.

DARIA

No, you can't, because in order for you to be non-monoga- mous you have to be having sex with even one person, for starters, right?

Ely is not amused.

DARIA

As for your hipness, I guess the new haircut helps.

Ely stops for a moment, fiddling with the white T-shirt in hand. She final- ly addresses Daria directly.

ELY

Who needs hipness. You know Max?

DARIA

Yeah, she's a total babe. What did you guys end up doing that night?

ELY

We went to a movie, we talked, it was nice.

Daria hops on top of the dryer as she prepares to hear some dirt.

DARIA

So, what happened? Did you go for it? I think she's totally hot.

ELY

(disappointedly)

I'm sure you think she's hot, Daria. And no I didn't go for it. I mean, you know, having a ball and chain in a far away place and being generally petrified of any interaction except for dogs, cats and an occa-

120 ✠

sional ferret doesn't exactly make me the hottest commodity around.

Ely throws some powder into the washer and shuts the lid. She leans on the machine and continues her conversation.

                    DARIA

          You're digging your own grave, girl—and you didn't answer me—do you like her?

                    ELY

          She seems kind of young. But, she probably only tried to kiss me out of boredom...

Ely taps Daria's legs, and she moves them away from the door of the dryer. Ely begins to pull clothes out and fold them.

                    DARIA

          So she "tried" to kiss you? Did she fail? Did you guys smooch, did she hump your leg—what happened?

                    ELY

          One lame kiss. Then Kate called. Let's just drop it. I mean I don't even . . .

Ely stops folding clothes for a moment.

                    DARIA

          Wanna deal with it? I think I'll have a dinner party. But wait— have you guys talked, or is it kind of weird?

                    ELY

          Well, we ran into each other the other day, at the bookstore. We had a conversation, but we didn't really talk about the date. Well, we talked about the date, but not really about kissing or anything. So, maybe it's a kind of weird.

Ely finishes her task and resumes leaning on the washer.

                    DARIA

          No, I think I'll throw a dinner party, and you're invited, and I'll invite a whole bunch of other hot babes, and it'll turn into a massive orgy. It'll be fabulous . . .

                              ELY

Whatever . . .

                              DARIA

Will you come?

                              ELY

Sure.

                              DARIA

                         (typically)

Will you cook?

                              ELY

                         (typically)

Fine.

                              DARIA

Do you still love me?

Ely grabs the bottom of Daria's shorts and tugs a little.

                              ELY

        Of course I still love you. You know, you haven't . . . "done"
Max, have you?

Daria chuckles, hops off the dryer and gives Ely a little hug.

                              DARIA

Oooh., I think Ely has a crush . . .

BELLA'S LOFT (YET ANOTHER DARIA CONQUEST) - DAY

Music plays as the camera dollies around a large loft. It is a sunny day
and Ely is cooking. The camera continues dollying to reveal Daria in bed
with Bella, having sex. While the music plays, various images with food
being prepared are intercut with Daria and Bella having sex. Finally a

finally a teapot whistles as daria has an **orgasm**

teapot whistles as Daria has an orgasm.

                    CUT TO:

INT. LOFT - LATER THAT DAY

Daria and Bella are getting dressed. Bella comes round the skimpy divider that separates the bed area from the kitchen, where Ely has been slaving away.

                    BELLA

        I'm going to the store to get some wine— would you like anything?

Ely is at the table chopping some vegetables.

                    ELY

    No, thanks.

Bella turns to leave, she stops for a moment and turns back to Ely.

                    BELLA

    Ely, thanks for cooking.

                    ELY

    No problem.

In the meantime Daria has entered the kitchen and is in the background getting a glass of water. She crosses over to where Ely is cooking and pats her on the shoulder.

                    DARIA

    Hey girl—how's it going?

                    ELY

    It's going OK.

                    DARIA

    You need any help?

Before Ely can answer, Daria is heading for the phone. She dials a number and begins to leave a message. Ely shakes her head and continues cooking.

                              DARIA

        Hi, it's Daria. Listen, I wanted to double check and see if you're still coming. Yeah, your answering machine cut me off. Yeah, we're here cooking a fabulous meal . . .

At this, Ely shoots Daria a look of disbelief. Daria is oblivious.

                              DARIA

        OK—see you then.

                         CUT TO:

INT. LOFT - LATER - EVENING

Ely is putting on her party shirt, when the doorbell rings, she begins to get it but Daria overtakes her.

124

                    DARIA

That's OK girl, I got it.

Daria opens the door to reveal Alice and Andy, the first of the dinner guests.

                    DARIA

Hey!

                    ALICE AND ANDY

Hi.

Daria embraces each woman and leads them over to where Ely stands.

                    DARIA

Come on in. Look who's here.

Alice is the first to get to Ely, she can't believe the haircut. She hugs Ely and rubs her head.

                    ALICE

Oh my God!

                    ELY

Hi Alice.

Just when Alice gets done rubbing Ely's head, Andy takes over, equally shocked over Ely's transformation.

                    ANDY

Is it you?

                    ELY

Hi Andy.

                    ALICE

Wow.

can i touch it?

ANDY

Check it out. Can I touch it?

DARIA

I'll get you guys a drink.

CUT TO:

INT. LOFT - MOMENTS LATER

The doorbell is heard and Daria answers it. It is Evy, alone, and Daria
immediately begins to flirt with her.

DARIA

Hi gorgeous.

EVY

Hi Daria.

DARIA

Welcome.

EVY

Thank you.

Daria leads her through the space and introduces her to Alice and Andy
who are seated in the living room.

DARIA

This is Alice and Andy.

EVY

Hi.

Ely approaches the two.

DARIA

Have you met Ely?

EVY

No. Hi, I'm Evy.

They shake, Evy seems a bit embarrassed, she is fully aware that they are all there to try and finally get Ely and Max together.

ELY

It's good to finally met you, Evy.

EVY

Likewise - I've heard a lot about you.

ELY

Well, Kia's told me some things about you.

In the background, Bella has returned from the store. She carries a bag with several bottles of wine. She approaches the group of women.

BELLA

(to Evy)

Hello, I'm Bella—I live here.

EVY

Hi I'm Evy. It's a nice place.

BELLA

Thanks. I'm gonna put this wine in the kitchen.

Bella exits frame and heads for the kitchen.

DARIA

Where's Kia?

EVY

She's parking the car—she'll be here.

Ely seems to be growing increasingly nervous, as most of the guests

have arrived except for Max.

                    ELY

        Is she alone?

                    DARIA

        Yeah—is Max with her?

                    EVY

        Max left a little before we did—I'm surprised she's not here.

                    ELY
                (dispassionately)
        I just need to know how much pasta to cook.

Ely runs back to the kitchen.

                    DARIA

        Ely's a little stressed. She's been cooking all day.

                    EVY

        Seems like it.

        CUT TO:

INT. LOFT - MOMENTS LATER

Ely busies herself in the kitchen as Kia enters the frame. She carries a six-pack of beer.

         KIA

  Hi Ely.

Ely is slightly startled and turns around quickly, embracing Kia.

         ELY

  Kia—Hi!

         KIA

  How are you doing?

         ELY

  Nice to see you.

         KIA

  I'm sorry—I didn't mean to startle you.

         ELY

  I didn't hear anyone come in.

         KIA

  Here—I brought this for the party,

Kia hands her the beer.

         ELY

  Oh, thanks.

         KIA

  I like your hair.

         ELY

  Oh, you haven't seen it yet.

Ely self-consciously rubs her head. The two women continue talking as the camera dollies away from them. They fall into the background as Daria and Evy come into the foreground. Daria puts her arm around Evy's waist and moves in close.

DARIA

So, how are you?

EVY

I'm good.

DARIA

I'm glad you came.

EVY

Don't flirt with me.

Evy removes Daria's hand. Daria does not miss a beat, and attempts to replace it.

DARIA

What—I'm just letting you know I still care.

Again, Evy removes Daria's hand from her waist.

EVY

Daria, I don't want to relive my past mistakes.

Again, Daria moves in.

DARIA

You had fun, you have to admit.

In the background Kia approaches the two women. Evy sees her and quickly puts her arms around her, kissing her hello.

EVY

I don't remember.

KIA

Hey girl, I see your moves.

DARIA

I was just about to make introductions.

Daria slinks off toward the living room.

                    KIA

    Shameless, she's absolutely shameless. Hi.

Kia and Evy kiss, still shaking their heads at Daria.

            CUT TO:

INT. LOFT - MOMENTS LATER

We see a group of women sitting around drinking and socializing, all
that is, but Ely. Bella enters frame and brings the news everyone was
waiting for.

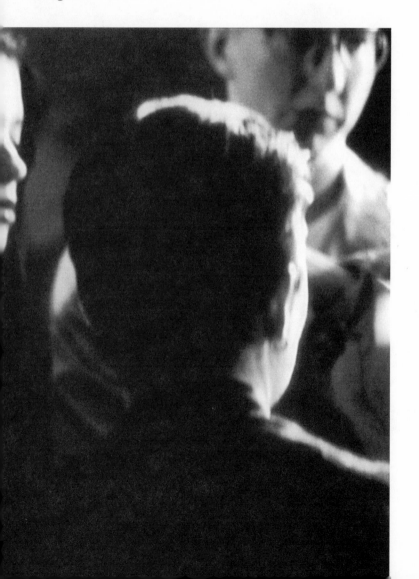

BELLA

Max is here.

EVY

Great.

Kia gets up to greet the tardy Max. Daria has also popped up to greet Max.

KIA

It's about time.

MAX

Shut up. (addressing Daria) Hi, sorry I'm late. Here, I bought these.

Max hands Daria a six-pack of tall boys and a pitcher of iced tea. Daria eyeballs them both and shamelessly flirts.

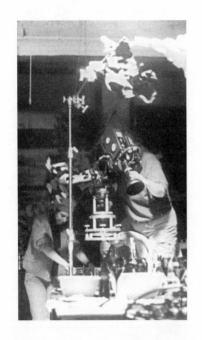

DARIA

Tall boys, for me? Iced tea. Who knew you were so healthy?

MAX

It's for Ely.

As Max embarrassingly admits this, Ely approaches.

DARIA

She brought you a present.

Daria quickly exits, leaving Ely and Max standing in the middle of the living room.

ELY

Hi Max. How are you?

MAX

Sorry I'm late. I'm fine.

ELY

That's all right.

They can't help but giggle. Ely contains herself and turns toward the group.

ELY

Umm, Max is here and we were just kind of waiting on her, so we can eat now.

CUT TO:

INT. LOFT KITCHEN - SOME TIME LATER

Music plays, and the remains of dinner is on the table. The camera pans over open wine and half-eaten pasta. The camera moves into the living room. All the women sit around the couches and chairs looking quite content and conversing. Daria is heard off camera.

DARIA

Another tall boy, Max?

MAX

No thanks, I'm fine.

Daria enters the frame, takes a seat and calls the women to attention. They are about to play a drinking game.

DARIA

OK, alright girls.

The chatter dies down and all the women turn their attention to Daria.

DARIA

I'll start off easy. I never . . . had sex with anyone in this room.

KIA

I can drink? OK.

All the women, with the exception of Ely and Max take a swig. It is now Kia's turn.

i'll start off easy. i never... had sex with anyone in this room.

alright... i've never fallen in love at first sight.

135

KIA

Okay. I've never had sex on a train that stopped because of an accident in the rain . . .

Everyone heckles at the length and believability of Kia's story.

ELY

How long is this story?

EVY

And then you woke up.

DARIA

If it wasn't for the rain part, I would have been drinking along with you.

Kia cheers with Daria and takes a hearty sip of her beer.

i've never called out the wrong names during sex.

EVY

A couple of studs—oh my God.

ELY

OK Evy . . .

EVY

Alright . . . I've never fallen in love at first sight.

Evy moves in close to Kia, they both take sips of their drinks and kiss. Max rolls her eyes.

MAX

Live with it, hate it.

DARIA

Did it.

ANDY

Come on, someone say something that I've done before—I need a drink.

GUEST

For real.

DARIA

Go Max—the pressure is on.

Silence as Max thinks. She looks up. She looks down.

MAX

Okay. Does it have to be about sex?

ELY

I don't think it has to.

ANDY

It's more fun.

ELY

(reassuringly)

It doesn't have to.

GUEST

Are you two a couple?

DARIA

Couple of geeks!

Everyone laughs except Ely and Max who seem vaguely horrified by the inquiry.

ELY & MAX

No—no we're not a couple.

MAX

Okay, I have one—I've never turned in a paper late.

Max takes a hearty sip and tries to ignore the hissing.

MAX

Hey—if Kia can brag, I can brag.

ANDY

Well, I got to drink anyway.

KIA

There you go.

ANDY

Ummm . . . I've never been having sex with someone and really wanted to change the music.

or we could just move right into spin the bottle.

EVY

Alright, it's gotta happen once.

GUEST

I've never called out the wrong name during sex.

Evy drinks again, while Kia explains it was not with her.

EVERYONE

Oooh Evy?

DARIA

Is that your girlfriend?

Finally it is Ely's turn. She wants the answer to the question that is still on her mind.

ELY

I've never had sex with Daria.

Evy takes another swig, Kia looks on shocked.

                    KIA

Hey.

Max has also taken a sip, along with about three other women at the party. Ely looks shocked and slightly disappointed.

                    OTHERS

Wow. Hey.

                    DARIA

Max, how could I have forgotten about that beautiful night?

                    MAX

Wait—someone tell me the rules?

                    KIA

Yeah, what are the rules? (to Evy) You just drank—I hope you were just thirsty.

                    ELY

Max, if you have done it.

MAX

Oh—I keep thinking you drink if you've never.

ELY

Maybe I should just ask the question over again?

KIA

Yeah, just ask it again.

Evy would like the confusion to get her off the hook.

EVY

No—I don't want to play anymore.

DARIA

Or we could just move right into spin the bottle.

Max is adamant about clearing the issue up.

MAX

Wait a minute! I never did it with Daria.

Evy admits it, to a very surprised Kia.

EVY

Okay, I admit it. It was a mistake.

ELY

(flatly)

It's always a mistake.

BELLA

Wait a minute—so you've slept with me, you slept with her, her and her?

Bella says this while pointing to various women in the room.

MAX

No! No! Not me!

She slaps her hand on the ground for emphasis.

DARIA

Hey! I don't deserve this abuse.

Daria stands up to her own defense.

DARIA

Look girls, I am a woman who loves women. Who wants to dance?

Daria exits the room.

CUT TO:

INT. LOFT LIVING ROOM AREA - LATER THAT NIGHT

Daria has passed out and is sleeping on Bella, who does not seem surprised. Ely and Max sit closely chatting for a long time. Finally, most of the guests leave. Ely and Max begin cleaning up. Ely stands in front of the sink washing dishes and Max stands next to her drying. The evening is almost over. Ely hands Max a dish.

ELY

So, what do ya think—did you have a pretty good time?

MAX

Yeah, it was fun. Daria seems a little drunk.

ELY

Daria's a little crazy.

Max nervously dries the dish in her hand. There is a slight silence as Ely stands smiling.

MAX

So do you wanna hang out some time? Like, I don't know, go

✄ 141

to a movie, or you know something, again?

                    ELY

              (nervous excitement)

That would be good. That would be fun.

                    MAX

I should give you my number.

                    ELY

I have your number.

                    MAX

                  (surprised)

You have my number?

                    ELY

Umm, it's Kia's number.

                    MAX

Oh, yeah.

Max finally puts the dish down and stands there holding the towel, shifting her weight, looking up and down. Ely is pretty awkward as well, but finds the nerve in herself to grab the towel from Max (as if she were going to dry her hands) bringing Max with it. They kiss by the sink.

On the other side of the apartment Kia has noticed Ely and Max. She leans over to the sleeping Daria and wakes her.

KIA

Daria! Look!

DARIA

All right!

The women high five, grinning from ear to ear at a job well done.

MAX'S APARTMENT / ELY'S APARTMENT

Max sits in her apartment talking on the phone with Ely. Simultaneously, Ely is lounging on the couch in her apartment, talking with Max.

MAX

It's West, Max West. Don't you think that's cool? Yeah, like can't you just picture me busting through the doors of a saloon in the old west? You're diggin' it, right, you're into it. I can tell. Cause that's my name—you know, as in—to the Max.

ELY

No, I mean that's not what your parents named you, right.

MAX

No, they named me Camille.

ELY

Umm . . . Torgeson.

MAX

No, no, they got divorced when I was like twelve, and now my Mom is like the stylin' single babe. He's cool—I don't see him that

you had a girl-
friend in high
school? that is
so totally cool.

much. I'm the baby, of course. The special one—the rest of them don't really matter. That's what I always tell my Mom anyway.

ELY

Only child. Yeah, I don't know what that means—there's some psychology about that, uh-huh. What would that smell like?

MAX

You had a girlfriend in high school? That is so totally cool.

ELY

Yeah, well it really wasn't that great because we weren't out to anyone except ourselves sort of, and not even, but we used to fight in the halls all the time, but we never kissed in the halls or anything, but people still called us lezzies.

MAX

Boys? Well, no, I was kind of, uh . . . Well there was this one boy that I dated for like three months, we didn't really date, we just held hands and talked about "My Three Sons" a lot because that was our favorite show. Just kinda dancing a lot and writing stuff for the news-paper. I don't know—I was kind of a geek. Still am, I guess.

Max is taking off her signature baseball cap and letting her hair down while she talks to Ely.

ELY

Well I did it when I brought Kate home once, because other-wise I didn't think my Mom would believe it—you know—she would just gloss it over, like so many other things. And she did anyway, I mean she hardly ever brings it up—I bring it up and she won't talk about it. But at least I know that she knows.

MAX

Okay, so tell me if this is totally rude and nosy, but I'm kind of curious—are you and Kate broken up now, or what's the story on that one?

Ely squirms a bit, and giggles nervously.

ELY

Well, we're sort of broken up. I mean—I left a message on

144 ⋈

her machine.

MAX

You left a message on her machine? So do you consider that broken up?

ELY

Yeah. She hasn't called me back yet. Yeah, well—it's half. I mean we're breaking up anyway, but we just need to talk about it.

MAX

So, like, that's 50/50—like you're broken up, she's not. But it counts for you, so I guess it counts for me then. I guess so.

Both women happily laugh.

NON-SPACE - NON-TIME

Three women lie on the floor with their backs to the camera. They are playing cards. Off-camera someone enters the room. It is Kia, and she's late. She hurries in and takes her position. All the women turn over onto their backs and face the camera. They are here to comment on the progress of Ely and Max. The mood is exhilarated.

KIA

Hi. Sorry I'm late—what are you guys playing?

ALICE

Go Fish.

KIA

Figures.

KIA

Hi—and you are?

DELLA

Della.

honey pot. never underestimate the power of a woman that's been deprived of the honey pot. never underestimate the power of a woman that's been deprived of the honey pot. never underestimate the power of a woman that's been deprived of the honey pot. never underestimate the power of a woman that's been deprived of the honey pot. never underestimate the power of a woman that's been deprived of the honey pot. never underestimate the power of a woman that's been deprived of the honey pot. never underestimate the power of a woman that's been deprived of the honey pot. never underestimate the power of a woman that's been deprived of the honey pot. never underestimate the power of a woman that's been deprived of the honey pot. never underestimate the power of a woman that's been deprived of the honey pot. never underestimate the power of a woman that's been deprived of the honey pot. never underestimate the power of a woman that's been deprived of the honey pot. never

vagina's
out.

KIA

But I can call you Del, right?

DELLA

No, Della.

KIA

Okay. Della.

Kia laughs.

DARIA

So you guys, how long do you think it'll be before they con-
summate?

KIA

Is that really the most important topic at hand? I'm just glad
our work is over finally.

DARIA

Well, y'all knowing Ely, it's gonna be at least two or three more
dates.

Sighs of disbelief, all around.

KIA

Two or three more dates—what is this, the lesbian Gandhi? I
don't have that kind of time to wait.

love
mound's
my
personal
fave.

EVY

Not everyone jumps right in, Kia.

DARIA

Yeah, come on, Kia, from "I sort of broke up with my girlfriend"
to "Let's fuck?" Not these babes.

KIA

Never underestimate the power of a woman that's been
deprived of the honey pot.

146 ⌦

DARIA

(shocked)

The honey pot?!

EVY

That honey pot thing has got to go.

DARIA

Yeah.

KIA

What do you guys call it? Come up with a more endearing term and I'll gladly put honey pot on the shelf.

EVY

I guess if you want endearing then vagina's out.

KIA

Yes nurse. Daria?

DARIA

Love mound's my personal fave.

Kia waves off this possibility.

KIA

Too Victorian.

DARIA

No it's not—picture this "Oh baby—you're so hot, I can't wait to get you home and pump your love mound."

EVY

Works for me.

KIA

Worked for you.

girlpatch.

how about cunt?

bearded clam?

General 'oohs' from the other women, but all is in good humor.

                              KIA

It's too euphemistic.

                              EVY

Girlpatch.

                              DARIA

Yeah!

                              KIA

Cute, but...is it sexy?

                              EVY

It can be, it can be.

Daria begins to act out her definition.

                              DARIA

        Let's see..."She moaned, grabbing her girlpatch in ecstasy..."
It works! I like it.

                              DEL

No, girlpatch sounds like a bad haircut.

                              DARIA

Well how about cunt?

                              KIA

No no no.

                              EVY

Way too harsh.

Daria makes an "L" sign with her thumb and index finger.

i love fish. fish is cute.

                    DARIA

    Losers. How about . . . Hmmm, let's see . . . bearded clam?

Kia and Evy laugh.

                    KIA

That's too high school locker room.

                    EVY

    Besides, there are people who get offended by that whole
bearded clam/fish thing.

                    DELLA

I love fish. Fish is cute.

                    EVY

I don't understand it. It doesn't taste like fish to me.

By now all the women are giggling, except Della who seems to be taking the entire conversation seriously.

                    DARIA

Something more in the line of the french fry family.

                    DELLA

It depends who you're with—now, you taste like—

Della is touching Daria on the head.

                    EVY

Oh, cut it out!

                    KIA

    Now, isn't honey pot sounding better and better? Sexy with-
out being vulgar, appealing with out being cutesy...

                    DARIA

    How 'bout just plain old "beav?" It's familiar, friendly, some-
thing you could almost say to Mom.

how bout just plain old beav?

im sticking with honeypot.

so is the the part where you ask me out on a date?

Laughter all around.

                    EVY

        I don't like the teeth.

                    KIA

        I'm sticking with honey pot.

ELY'S APARTMENT / MAX'S APARTMENT

The telephone scene continues.

                    MAX

        So, is this the part where you ask me out on a date?

                    ELY

            (shyly)

        Umm . . . would you like to go on a date with me?

                    MAX

            (bashfully)

        I would love to go on a date with you— what do you want to
do?

                    ELY

        Umm—I don't know, I hadn't got that far— what do you wanna
do?

                    MAX

        Well, we already saw a movie . . . Why don't you just come
over, and we'll just figure it out.

KIA AND MAX'S APARTMENT - SLIGHTLY LATER THAT EVENING

Max sits on the couch and waits impatiently for the bathroom to be free. Kia and Evy are in the shower, and the emphasis is not on clean-

liness. Max decides to decorate the house while she is waiting. A sweet song begins to play. Max is done decorating and is sitting at the kitchen table still waiting for the bathroom. Finally she hears the sounds of life as Kia and Evy emerge sheepishly from the bathroom.

                    EVY

    Sorry Max—have we been in there too long?

Max shoots her a look.

                    KIA

    You know, we probably saved you a lot of time by showering together.

Max gets up and heads for the bathroom.

                    EVY

    It's her big date.

Evy runs off to the bedroom. Kia hangs around looking at the trans-formed apartment. She is amused, Max is not.

                    KIA

    I see that you've turned the place into a den of love.

Max is quiet as she enters the bathroom.

                         KIA

         So—what are you guys gonna do?

                         MAX

              (frustrated)

         Kia, That's the thing—I don't even know, she's gonna be here
in ten minutes and I am not even dressed.

                         KIA

         Don't have sex in our bed.

                         MAX

              (appalled)

         We're not gonna do it.

INT. BOTH APARTMENTS - EVENING

Everyone is preparing to go out. The same song heard at the beginning
of the scene rises again as Ely tries to pick out the perfect outfit. Cut
to Daria in the bathroom getting dressed, putting on her boots, jacket,
rings and some lipstick. Cut to Kia and Evy getting dressed. Kia puts on
her signature blazer and Evy tries to get her to not wear it for just a
night. Cut back to Ely who is playing with her hair, trying on a cap forward then backward. Kia and Evy finish dressing and take some time
for hugs and kisses. Ely stands in the doorway, waiting for inspection.
Daria enters the frame, straightening a couple of things on Ely. She has
an idea. She exits the frame and returns, carrying a bag. It is a safe
sex kit. She hands it to Ely, who hands it back. Daria insists that Ely
take it.

INT. MAX'S APARTMENT - LATER THAT EVENING

Kia and Evy have left for the evening. Max is still in the bathroom when
Ely enters the frame. She quietly walks up to the bathroom door and
knocks, tentatively.

MAX

Go away please!

ELY

Max, it's Ely. I just wanted to tell you that I'm here.

MAX

Hi Ely!

Max quickly throws open the door. She stands in the doorway with a robe on, and for the first time Ely sees Max without her cap on.

MAX

You're early.

ELY

Yeah.

MAX

Oh no, it's me, I'm late. What time is it?

ELY

Don't worry.

MAX

Umm—I'll be out in a second.

Ely smiles reassuringly. Max closes the door of the bathroom. Ely wanders around the kitchen. She removes a picture from the refrigerator, which is a picture of Max's parents that Max placed there while she was decorating. The bathroom door opens and Max emerges to find Ely with the picture in hand.

MAX

Hey don't look at that.

Ely chuckles and holds up the photograph.

                    ELY

          Your parents?

                    MAX

          Yeah. Kinda geekin' I guess.

                    ELY

          Funny picture.

Ely carefully replaces the picture and follows Max as she walks into the
living room.

                    MAX

          How did you get in here?

                    ELY

          Kia and Evy were on their way down and they let me up.

                    MAX

               Kia is always doing that shit to me. She wanted me to walk
          out here in my skivvies and have you standing in the middle of the liv-
          ing room.

Ely laughs, she knows this is true of Kia. She follows Max, who stops
her before her bedroom.

                    MAX

          Oh—you can just sit right there—I'm gonna get dressed.

Ely sits on the couch, waiting. Max comes out of her room a moment
later, still in her robe. She takes a seat next to Ely, looks at her and
gives her a kiss hello.

                    MAX

          You look nice.

                    ELY

          Thanks.

Max is up again. Ely just watches her.

                    MAX

        I'm gonna put on some music.

Music begins. Ely waits. Max emerges from her room, still in her robe.
She carries two shirts. She comes in and sits next to Ely again.

                    MAX

        I'm sorry I'm not ready—I'm just having the inevitable fashion
crisis.

                    ELY

        I know what you mean.

Max displays both shirts for Ely.

MAX

Okay, which one do you think I should wear? I've got this one with the three on it—I think it's kind of cool, this one's a little bit crazy.

Ely feels both shirts. While she is doing this Max looks at her fingers, specifically her nails.

ELY

This fabric's nice. You should wear this one.

MAX

Oh my God look at your nails! Sorry— that's really rude.

Max jumps up from the couch. She is embarrassed, but probably not as much as Ely. She tries to regroup.

MAX

Okay—this one?

ELY

(absentmindedly)

Yeah.

MAX

I'll wear it.

Max exits quickly, leaving Ely on the couch looking at her fingernails.

ELY

Hey if you have some clippers I'll cut them right now . . .

Max comes back to the living room.

MAX

Oh, you're really gonna cut 'em?

ELY

Yeah.

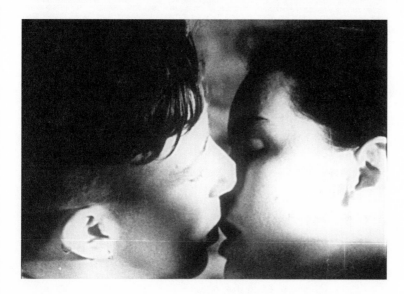

Ely stands up. They stand very close to each other as Max tries to explain.

                    MAX

    In the bathroom, there's this ceramic thing . . .

                    ELY

        (clueless)

    Okay, a ceramic thing?

                    MAX

    Yeah—

                    MAX

    I'll get 'em. Sit down

Max puts her hand on Ely's shoulder and sits her back down. She goes to the bathroom to get the clippers. She returns, handing Ely the clippers, then returns to her bedroom to get dressed.

                    ELY

    Thanks.

Ely begins to cut her nails. She is having some difficulty.

kiss

kiss

kiss

 ely

and

kiss

kiss

max kiss

kiss kiss

start

kiss

kiss

kiss to

kiss kiss kiss

kiss

kiss kiss

kiss

kiss kiss

kiss kiss

kiss kiss

kiss

kiss kiss kiss

kiss kiss

ELY

Hey is there something wrong with these? They make my nails all sharp and everything.

Max emerges from her bedroom, robe still on. She gives Ely a tap on the knee and sits close to her.

MAX

Here, move over—they're toenail clippers so there's kind of an art to making them work.

Max takes Ely's hand and prepares to cut her nails. She picks a finger, but Ely has already cut that nail, edges pointy.

MAX

I see you tried on that one.

Max picks another nail and tries to cut it.

MAX

Oooh.

Ely smiles, being supportive. She is enjoying this moment. They both laugh.

ELY

It works.

MAX

They're not really that long except they have these sharp edges.

ELY

From the clippers.

Moments later, Max has leaned back and Ely seems more relaxed.

MAX

Okay, I'm almost done. I don't know why I made such a big deal out of it, I guess they're really not that long.

                    ELY

    It's all right.

Ely kisses Max on the neck. Max is surprised, in a good way.

                    MAX

    Bold.

Ely and Max start to kiss. They continue to kiss as the camera does a series of pans. Pan left, they are kissing. Pan right they are on top of each other. Pan left, they are sleeping. Pan right, it is morning, Ely is up getting dressed. Max sleeps. Ely pulls the sheet up over her, kisses her and exits.

EXTERIOR - VARIOUS LOCATIONS - MORNING

A happy mambo tune kicks in as Ely goes home. She is overjoyed. She skips down the alley, tosses her keys in the air. Spins a complete stranger in the middle of the street and gets a flower from the flower vendor. Finally she approaches her home. As she tiptoes through her house the music fades down. She rounds the corner and is about to go into the bathroom when . . .

DARIA AND ELY'S APARTMENT - MORNING

daria
runs
off
camera
and
grabs
a sign
she
has
made.
it is a
large
heart,
which
reads
"ely &
max".

DARIA

Good Morning, Sunshine!

Daria is standing in the kitchen, glass of tea in hand. This is the moment she's been waiting for.

ELY

(trying to be cool)

Oh, hi Daria—hey—how come you're still up?

DARIA

(feigning concern)

I was worried sick about you . . .

Ely takes a seat at the table. Daria comes and stands above her.

ELY

I'm sorry, I should have called or something.

DARIA

I was wondering—what could she be doing? Maybe locked out, but no, I was here...working a double shift at the vet's office? Maybe hangin' out all night again at the S&M dungeon? Or could she have been spending time with one Max West?

Ely looks sheepish.

ELY

Yes, I was with Ms. West.

DARIA

(excitedly)

God—it's true! Really? I made something for you.

Daria runs off camera and grabs a sign she has made. It is a large heart, which reads "Ely & Max". Ely giggles.

                        ELY

    That's really cute, Daria.

                        DARIA

    Made it with my own two hands. You like?

Daria brings the sign to the table and hands it to Ely.

                        ELY

    It's really nice, thanks.

        CUT TO:

INT. KIA AND MAX'S APARTMENT - MORNING

Kia and Evy sit on either side of Max, who has just woken up and is still
wrapped in a sheet.

                        KIA

        So, this is where it all happened, huh? It's a good thing we
came home so late.

Max butts into Kia.

EVY

How was it, Max? Was it like losing your virginity all over again?

Max smiles in an "I'll never tell" way.

KIA

(impatiently)

So?

MAX

So what?

KIA

Come on, give us the dirt!

Max smiles and gives in.

MAX

It was great.

EVY

(impatiently)

More dirt than that.

CUT TO:

INT. DARIA AND ELY'S APARTMENT - MORNING

Daria moves to the other side of the table and sits down.

DARIA

So, tell, blow by blow, and don't skip any adverbs.

Ely looks very shy.

ELY

Daria, what do you want to know?

DARIA

I want to know how it started. Did you pin her down, did you slip her some Spanish fly?

CUT TO:

INT. MAX AND KIA'S APARTMENT

Max continues her story. Evy and Kia are riveted.

MAX

We never even went out.

KIA

Smooth—how'd ya swing that one?

MAX

(bragging)

I never even got dressed.

EVY

(impressed)

Ooh, girl.

Kia pats Max on the knee.

                    KIA

You know you owe me one for letting her in.

Max gives her a look.

                    EVY

    Alright, so you come out of the bathroom stark naked, and she is standing in the the middle of the room . . .

                    MAX

    No! I was wearing a bathrobe.

Kia and Evy are surprised.

                    KIA

    Max, I cannot believe how uptight you are. You're home alone and you don't walk around naked?

                    MAX

    No—I knew she was here. Your plan didn't work—she knocked on the door, so I didn't come out naked.

                    EVY

    So you open the door you're out, and she pounces on you like a wild animal . . .

Kia and Evy are in their own world, making up their own version of the story, almost completely forgetting about Max.

                    KIA

    And she wrestles you to the floor in a fit of passion . . .

                    EVY

    And you say "Ely we've just met. . ."

Max leans back and watches them go.

i never even got dressed.

KIA

And she says "I've wanted you from the moment I laid eyes on you . . ."

MAX

You guys.

Kia motions impatiently for Max to get on with it.

KIA

We know all that part, we want to know how it started.

MAX

Alright—she was sitting on the couch—she was sitting like, over there and she was cutting her nails . . .

CUT TO:

INT. DARIA AND ELY'S APARTMENT - CONTINUED

Daria has a look of disbelief on her face.

DARIA

You were cutting your nails? (pause) Do you usually tend to your personal hygiene on a first date? That's very hot, Ely.

ELY

(laughing)

It was . . .

CUT TO:

INT. MAX AND KIA'S APARTMENT - CONTINUED

MAX

. . . And then she needed help, and so I started cutting her nails for he . . .

Both Kia and Evy don't believe what they are hearing.

KIA

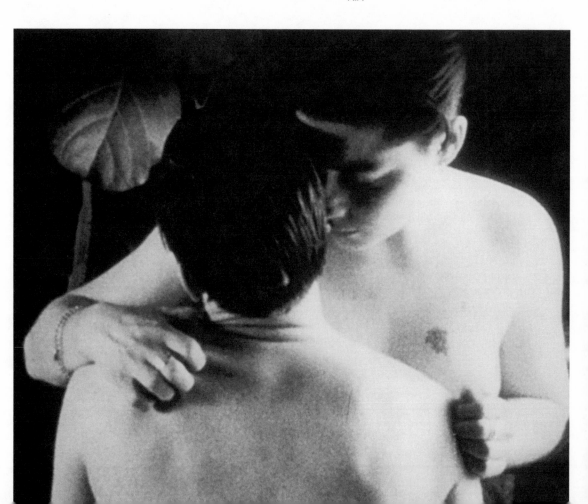

Wait a minute, wait, wait—I know it's been a really long time, but what kind of foreplay is nail cutting?

CUT TO:

FANTASY SEQUENCE

Kia and Evy imagine Max cutting Ely's nails. Max virginal, Ely lecherous. The sound track is very cheesy disco music.

CUT BACK TO:

WOMEN ON COUCH

Evy and Kia turn their attention back to Max.

EVY

I don't know, that sounds kind of sexy to me . . .

KIA

OK, OK, so I can see that, and?

CUT TO:

INT. ELY AND DARIA'S APARTMENT - CONTINUED

ELY

She was making fun of my nails, so I started cutting them, and then she came over and started cutting them for me . . . and, you know.

Daria looks off into space.

CUT TO:

FANTASY SEQUENCE

Daria imagines Max cutting Ely's nails. In Daria's fantasy, Max is a brazen hussy in a teddy and Ely is her prey.

CUT BACK TO:

ELY AND DARIA SITTING AT THE TABLE

Daria snaps out of her fantasy.

                    DARIA

        So, she cut your nails, and then..

                     ELY

        It was nice. We talked for a while and we were gonna go out,
but she couldn't decide what to wear—

                    DARIA

        Ely cut to the chase! I want details.

                CUT TO:

INT. MAX AND KIA'S APARTMENT - CONTINUED

                     MAX

        And so I'm cutting her nails, and then, she kind of kissed my
neck—right there and then . . .

                CUT TO:

INT. ELY AND DARIA'S APARTMENT - CONTINUED

                     ELY

        I was feeling a little out of practice, Daria-

Daria waves off Ely's fear.

                    DARIA

        It's like riding a bike—

                CUT TO:

INT. MAX AND KIA'S APARTMENT - CONTINUED

                     MAX

        . . . And we started kissing, and then . . .

                CUT TO:

INT. ELY AND DARIA'S APARTMENT - CONTINUED

                168   ⊙⋈

ELY

Well, we were on the couch, and we started kissing. . .

CUT TO:

INT. MAX AND KIA'S APARTMENT - CONTINUED

MAX

And I kinda straddled her—kinda like this . . .

Max pretends to straddle Kia.

CUT TO:

INT. DARIA AND ELY'S APARTMENT - CONTINUED

DARIA

(impressed)

On the couch? That takes some maneuvering . . .

Ely looks pretty proud of herself.

CUT TO:

INT. MAX AND KIA'S APARTMENT - CONTINUED

⋈

Max laughs giddily.

MAX

And then . . . you know—

CUT TO:

FLASHBACK - SEX SCENE - NIGHT

Music plays as we see images of Ely and Max, kissing, naked, moving, fucking.

CUT BACK TO:

MAX, EVY AND KIA ON THE COUCH

Max is looking pretty proud of herself. Kia and Evy are looking pretty proud of her too.

KIA

Wow.

Evy pats Max on the knee.

CUT TO:

DARIA AND ELY AT THE TABLE

Ely looks pretty proud of herself. Daria looks impressed.

DARIA

Wow. Congratulations.

ELY

Thanks.

Ely grins largely.

CUT TO:

WOMEN ON THE COUCH

EVY

Cool.

flashback
sex
sex
sex
scene
night

⋈ 171

Max throws her head back in laughter.

CUT TO:

DARIA AND ELY AT THE TABLE

Daria pauses for a moment and looks puzzled.

DARIA

So why didn't you stay?

Ely is sitting back in her chair in a mock-studly way.

ELY

Playing hard to get?

Daria shakes her head and smiles at Ely.

EXTERIOR - DAY

Very upbeat music begins as Ely and Max spend the day together. They sit by the lake and watch the waves, get coffee, walk around the north side of Chicago and hang out.

CUT TO:

INT. ELY AND DARIA'S APARTMENT - DAY

We see Daria approaching an open doorway, talking to Ely, who is not there.

DARIA

Ely—you'll never guess who I saw at the bar last night, girl.

Daria comes into the room and sees that it is empty.

DARIA

Hello? Man, you get a girlfriend, you're never home.

CUT BACK TO:

EXTERIOR - DAY

Ely and Max continue frolicking around outside.

CUT TO:

INT. MAX AND KIA'S APARTMENT - DAY

Kia walks through the door. She has just come home, she finds, to an empty house.

KIA

Hey, I'm home. Hello? Anybody home? Evy? Anybody?

CUT TO:

INTERIORS - EVENING

Ely and Max come home. They throw themselves on the bed prepared to sleep, but start to kiss instead. All of the other principle characters are shown heading in the same direction.

A woman stands by a door and Daria approaches her, grabbing her and kissing her.

Kia and Evy are in their bedroom kissing.

Continue to intercut between these three sex scenarios, while the music plays. The tempo gets increasingly fast as the sex gets more intense.

Finally Ely and Max are naked. Max is on top of Ely, moving up Ely's body towards her head. Ely grabs her head and brings their faces together for a kiss. They embrace, completely content. During this last segment there is a voice over.

Voice-over

Don't fear too many things—it's dangerous. Don't say so much— you'll ruin everything. Don't worry yourself into a corner and just don't think about it so much. The girl you're gonna meet doesn't look like anyone you know, and when you meet her, your toes might tingle, or you might suppress a yawn. It's hard to say. Don't box yourself in. Don't leave yourself wide open. Don't think about it every second, but just don't let yourself forget. The girl is out there.

Close on a grainy image of Ely and Max embracing.

THE END

END CREDITS ROLL AS MUSIC RISES

THE OVERLOOK PRESS

IN ASSOCIATION WITH

STEPHEN PEVNER, INC.

PRESENTS

A BOOK DESIGNED BY
PAUL WEST

EDITED BY
TRACY CARNS

BASED UPON THE MOVIE BY

THE SAMUEL GOLDWYN
COMPANY

ISLET PRESENTS

A CAN I WATCH PICTURES
PRODUCTION

IN ASSOCIATION WITH KVPI

PRODUCED BY
ROSE TROCHE
GUINEVERE TURNER

WRITTEN BY
GUINEVERE TURNER
ROSE TROCHE

EXECUTIVE PRODUCERS
TOM KALIN
CHRISTINE VACHON

GO FISH

DIRECTED BY
ROSE TROCHE

END CREDITS

CINEMATOGRAPHER
ANN T. ROSSETTI

ORIGINAL SCORE BY
BRENDAN DOLAN
JENNIFER SHARPE
WITH SCOTT ALDRICH

EDITOR
ROSE TROCHE

SOUND EDITOR
MISSY COHEN

DIALOGUE EDITOR
JACOB RIBICOFF

FEATURING

ELY
V.S. BRODIE

MAX
GUINEVERE TURNER

KIA
T. WENDY MCMILLAN

EVY
MIGDALIA MELENDEZ

DARIA
ANASTASIA SHARP

LIGHTING DIRECTORS
ANN T. ROSSETTI
ARTHUR C. STONE

SOUND RECORDISTS
LISA HUBBARD
ELSPETH KYDD

ASSISTANT DIRECTOR
WENDY QUINN

ASSOCIATE PRODUCER
V.S. BRODIE

ASSISTANT EDITORS
LISA HUBBARD/JESSE WEINER

ASSISTANT DIALOGUE EDITORS
GILLIAN CHI
KARL WASSERMAN

ASSISTANT CAMERA
KELLY KROTINE
JOE VIDAL
MIMI WADELL

ADDITIONAL CAMERA
JANE JEFFERES
ROSE TROCHE
JOE VIDAL

GAFFER
JOY CASTRO NOVA

ADDITIONAL LIGHTING
MAIDA SUSSMAN
ELSPETH KYDD

ADDITIONAL SOUND
JOE VIDAL
WALTER YOUNGBLOOD

FOLEY ENGINEER
GEORGE LARA

FOLEY ARTIST
BRIAN VANCHO

ADR ENGINEERS
GEORGE LARA/DAVID NOVAK

RE-RECORDING ENGINEER
DAVID NOVAK

ASSISTANT SOUND
JOE VIDAL
WALTER YOUNGBLOOD

WITH
(IN ORDER OF APPEARANCE)

STUDENT #1/JURY MEMBER
MARY GARVEY

STUDENT #2
JENNIFER ALLEN

STUDENT #3
WALTER YOUNGBLOOD

STUDENT #3/JURY MEMBER
DANIELA FALCON

STUDENT #4
ARTHUR C. STONE

ANGRY STUDENT
ELSPETH KYDD

STUDENT #5/JURY MEMBER
TRACY KIMME

MEL
BROOKE WEBSTER

MIMI
MIMI WADELL

HAIRCUTTER
SCOUT

BRIDE #1/JURY MEMBER
SUSAN GREGSON

BRIDE #2/JURY MEMBER
CAROLYN KOTLARSKI

BRIDE #3/JURY MEMBER
JOANNA BROWN

EVY'S MOTHER
BETTY JEANNE PEJKO

JUNIOR
ALFREDO TROCHE

SAM
JOANNE C. WILLIS

THE BOY
JONATHAN T. VINCENT

JURY MEMBER #1
JAMIKA AJALON

JURY MEMBER #2
MICHELE CULLOM

HERSELF
MARIANNA

BELLA
SHELLY SCHNEIDER BELLO

ALICE
STEPHANIE BOLES

ANDY
JULIA LAFLEUR

DINNER GUEST #1
LISA RAYMOND

DINNER GUEST #2
NIN VON VOSS

DELLA
DOROTHEA REICHENBACHER

ADDITIONAL CAST
AHNDI
LISA BALDASSARI
JACQUELINE BRISSET
VICTORIA BROWN
DEBRA CRAWFORD
SABRINA CRAIG
STEPHEN CRAIG
DAINTY
KEVIN M. GRUBB
ELIZABETH HERNANDEZ
PAMELA HEWETT
MARK HOUSTON
JEANNE KRACHER
KELLY KROTINE
OLGA LOPEZ
MELORA
JUAREZ MONACO
JENNIFER MORTON
JOANNE MORTON
RICK POWELL
WENDY QUINN
KAREN SPIES
ANN T. ROSSETTI
ROSE TROCHE
JOE VIDAL
SHANIQUA WASHINTON

ADDITIONAL VOICES
DERRICK KARDOS
JULIA ZAY
SUSAN STRINE
LAURA GERACE
MIRIAM GERACE GUARENA
GILLIAN CHI
KARL WASSERMAN
JACOB RIBICOFF
TOM KALIN

PRODUCTION ASSISTANTS
RICK POWELL
JOANNE MORTON

GRIPS
DEBBIE SNEAD
SARA VARON
REBECCA MCBRIDE
JAN COLLINS
WALTER YOUNGBLOOD
TRACY KIMME
OSCAR CERVERA
JOANNE MORTON
JOANNE BROWN
SCOUT
PAUL SHABAZ
KEVIN M. GRUBB
JENNIFER ALLEN
JOANNE WILLIS

BOOM OPERATORS
JENNIFER ALLEN
THERESA CASTINO
LISA GILLESPIE
KERRY HILGAR
MARY ELVA KOUKLIS
JEAN KRACHER
JULIA LAFLEUR
DIANE SWANSON
WALTER YOUNGBLOOD

DOLLY PUSHERS
KELLY KROTINE
SCOUT
JOE VIDAL
MIMI WADELL
JOANNE WILLIS
WALTER YOUNGBLOOD

SLATE
SABRINA CRAIG

CONTINUITY
RICK POWELL
LISA RAYMOND

TRANSPORTATION
KEVIN M. GRUBB
RICK POWELL

CATERING
MICHELE CULLOM
DANA ESHGHI
MARY GARVEY
SCOUT
MITCHELL STEVENS
TRACY KIMME
MARY ELVA KOUKLIS
MELORA
CANDACE RONDEAUX
BROOKE WEBSTER
ALFREDO TROCHE
JOHN DODGE
CHRISTOPHER MARTINEZ

LOCATIONS
QUIMBY'S QUEER STORE
GOLD STAR BAR
GREEN STREET CAFE
UNIVERSITY OF ILLINOIS, CHICAGO

ANIMALS
BELLA
RAT BASTARD, JR
SKEETER "MIRACLE KITTY"
STASH
TOBY

NEGATIVE CUTTER
TIM BRENNAN

OPTICAL EFFECTS
ROSE TROCHE

TITLES
GUINEVERE TURNER

BLACK AND WHITE PRINT BY
ALPHA CINE

SOUND MIXED AT
SOUND ONE

OPTICALS
MILLENIUM

BLACK AND WHITE PROCESSING
BPS PHOTO LABS
ALPHA CINE

ADDITIONAL FUNDING
FRAMELINE FILM AND VIDEO
COMPLETION FUND

"SOMEONE" WRITTEN BY
MILA DRUMKE
JENNIFER SHARPE

VOCALS/ACOUSTIC GUITAR
MILA DRUMKE

ACOUSTIC/ELECTRIC GUITAR
JENNIFER SHARPE

DRUMS
ALEXI HAWLEY

VIOLIN
TONY CROSS

BASS
MARC PALADIN

SPECIAL THANKS
JEANNE KRACHER
HANS SCHALL
PAUL SHUKIN
HENRIQUE CIRNE LIMA
MARY PATTEN
V.S. BRODIE
SUSAN STRINE
JAMES BURLING CHASE
CAROLEE PURCELL
HOLLIS RHODES
GERSHWIN THE WONDER DOG
CRAIG MEESON
MELISSA DUKE

THANKS TO
MARTIN NELSON
GALADRIELLE ALLMAN
SARA RYAN
DEBBIE GOULD
LYNETTE WOOD
JUSTIN BLOCK
STEPHEN JONES
CHRIS HILL
JOHN BRUCE
FLETCHER CHICAGO
SONIC BOOM
LEO'S LUNCHROOM
BERLIN
CAIRO
TEMPATIONS
VORTEX
JIMO'S
PARIS DANCE
ANN SATHER'S RESTAURANT
WINDY CITY TIMES
UNIVERSITY OF ILLINOIS
JOYCE GEORGE
THE GIRLS AT 49 ST. MARKS
BILL NISSELSON
THE SOUND ONE CREW
ELLEN KURAS
BUREAU NEW YORK
B. RUBY RICH
SANDE ZEIG
MARLENE MCCARTY
BRAGMAN NYMAN CAFARELLI